MINERAN
INFLUENCE

P N BURROWS

Mineran Influence
Book one of the Mineran Series

First published in 2015
P N Burrows

Copyright © P N Burrows 2016

ISBN-13: 978-1540536785

DEDICATION

For my parents who started me on the greatest adventure
there is: Living.

CONTENTS

CHAPTER 1

With a determined look, Sam took out a rather tatty-looking case from the flimsy bed-and-breakfast plywood wardrobe. The abuse of thousands of miles of travel disguised the fact that the case was actually an extremely expensive military grade valise. It would survive an air crash with nothing more than a few scratches and it would prove equally as tough to anyone trying to pry it open. Sam inserted an odd-looking key into the lock aperture and released the mechanism with a combination of his fingerprint and vocal key phrase. The combination of key, various fingerprints and phrases allowed for various security settings to be evoked. Sam had it set to either open, secure lockdown for one hour or secure lockdown for twenty-four hours. He didn't have, nor did he desire to have installed the more elaborate options of SOS call-out with GPS co-ordinates, secure thermite eradication of the contents or the release of various gaseous compounds depending on the desired outcome.

It was far beyond Sam's requirements and financial scope to purchase such a case. Matt Johnson had asked him to user-test the case and a smaller version over a year ago. It was part of Matt's new security portfolio for the one percent executives, and the final version could have a retina and finger vascular pattern verification as an optional upgrade.

With a solid-sounding clunk, the clasps opened, and Sam removed the smaller, sleeker black case from amongst his clothes. This particular case had arrived yesterday, upon his request to Matt, tattily wrapped and couriered to his B&B as a disguised eBay purchase.

Again he inserted the key, activated the barely visible print scanner with his little pinkie and carefully sang the first two lines from Louis Prima's 1946 swing classic, "'Just a Gigolo'", at the correct tempo of 127 beats per minute. Matt had programmed in seven swing classics which rotated on a daily basis. This was the lowest security setting, the most severe being a new passphrase for each day of the year. Matt had chosen classic swing tunes as his current girlfriend was an avid Lindy Hopper and her enthusiasm for the genre was rubbing off on him.

'Matt, you're a dick! Even with all of your money, you couldn't be a gigolo. More so now you've grown that hideous mouth brow.' During a scheduled maintenance inspection of the cases, Matt had let slip that the "test user" version recorded for sixty seconds after verification, to allow the beta tester to leave comments. Sam took advantage of this to frequently leave suggestive and semi-constructive comments for his close friend and quite possibly future employer. If nothing else, it would give the tech guys a laugh.

Sam carefully removed the items from the pre-moulded foam. He placed a Glock 20 on the bed alongside three empty magazines, a box of 10mm hollow-points, an adapted holster for concealed carry in his jacket, two finger-hooped throwing knives, a Kubaton disguised as a pen and a powerful LED pocket torch.

With slow but firm precision, he loaded 15 hollow-points into the magazines, having checked the tension in the springs first. A common rookie mistake was to leave the magazines loaded in storage, causing the spring tension to decrease with fatigue and consequently causing a jam at a most inconvenient time. Sam slowly inserted a magazine and cocked the weapon, the smell of the gun oil filling his nostrils as the first bullet entered the chamber. He ejected the magazine back into his hand to insert another round and then replaced it back into the butt of the Glock. Sam placed the gun in the holster and returned it to the bed.

He left the G29 backup pistol and ankle holster in the case along with the spare barrels and firing pins for each gun. He meticulously locked both cases and returned them to the wardrobe, draping the sleeve of his shirt across the top, the button aligned with a small stain as a simple tell in case of snoopers.

Donning his favourite tactical coat, a charcoal black jacket he had bought in the States, he started to load it up. This jacket was designed by his favourite garment manufacturer in collaboration with a bestselling thriller author. God knows why they chose an author to help with the design, but they came up with an impressive and usable nondescript carry system that was comfortable and practical. At only $200 off-the-shelf stateside, he considered it a bargain.

Being right-handed, Sam mounted the holster into the outside-left chest carry pocket, which made it float just below his left pectoral muscle. He'd had the pocket interior adjusted to mount the holster in the correct position for him. The two finely balanced throwing knives slid into the sleeve cuff pockets with ease. He always kept the adaptive sheaths inserted in the sleeves for convenience. The rest of the gear was stashed in the appropriate pockets, mostly indicated by little sewn-in pictogram labels.

Sam looked across the dimly lit room towards the bottle of Scotch whisky. It only contained a mouthful of what the Scots call "the water of life". The bottle was one of several concerns at the moment, but it was something that had troubled him more than the other odd things that had happened over the last few weeks. Its presence prompted an epiphany, a realisation that things were not right and a series of discoveries that had riled Sam's calm demeanour.

The previous Saturday, he had attempted to walk from his cheap boarding that was situated just outside the old tired market town of Wrexham, intending to traverse over the relatively small mountain in Minera. He "came to" wandering a trail a few miles further along carrying the aforementioned bottle, feeling groggy, his breath stinking of whisky and with a headache from hell. Whilst he was no newcomer to hangovers, he seldom drank to excess anymore and never whilst out walking.

In fact, he only ever drank whisky in memory of fallen friends and comrades on the anniversary of their passing. This was his old squad's tradition that would stay with him for the rest of his life. The harsh taste as he drank a shot for each friend he'd lost was not just caused by his dislike for whisky, but due to the loss and emptiness he felt every time. With over twenty years of service behind him, he had lost quite a few good friends. Four nights ago he had toasted Corporal Danny Burgess's life, lost in a needless skirmish in the first year of Sam's active duty.

Personal body armour will only protect certain parts of

your body; mobility and weight being key factors in what you can or cannot wear for different scenarios. Danny took a bullet across his exposed windpipe from a robed adversary that sprung up from behind a wall, spraying bullets randomly like a 1920s TV gangster. Others popped up from ravines and from behind the ramshackle buildings. Far from the frontline, on the outskirts of a liberated and supposedly safe village, this was not the welcome the squad had anticipated.

Danny bled out in front of Sam quickly, although at the time it had seem like an eternity as Sam tried to staunch the flow with his hands. Crimson red froth bubbled out from between Sam's fingers and out of Danny's mouth and nose as he was simultaneously dying from exsanguination and asphyxiation. The fear in Danny's eyes mirrored Sam's. Slowly, the spark of life faded and Danny's hands that had been gripping so hard, almost as if he could hold on to Sam he could hold on to life, released and fell to the floor, creating a puff of dust that then settled and mingled with the arterial spray. Danny had died and the tremendous sound of the battle continued on around them, but it hadn't drowned out the horrendous gurgling sound of his last breath. The rest of the squad had supplied covering fire whilst Sam had tried to treat their fallen comrade.

Sam's senses came back to the battle at hand. He now heard the short controlled bursts of suppression fire from the LSW and shorter bursts from SA80s. The louder barks of Kalashnikovs faltered, as did the sound of bullets impacting all around. Their ambushers were poorly trained and most had fired off the majority of their ammunition within the first minute of the ambush. Torsos and heads popped out of cover to fire gangland style, AKs held away from the torso or from the hip, allowing the recoil to raise the barrel up.

The rest of the squad survived the badly orchestrated ambush intact. A much younger and inexperienced Sam acted on the procedures that the constant training of the military ingrained into him for just such an occasions: through muscle memory formed by constant rigorous combat scenarios, learnt by rote, designed solely to get you through such situations. Between that and the organisation skills that were barked from Sargent Trooper, a most unfortunate name for a soldier, and sheer bloody willpower to avenge the death of their friend, they overcame the aggressors.

At the end there was a body count of twelve, including Danny and three badly wounded attackers. None of them looked old enough to shave, let alone handle an automatic rifle. Amid rather harsh questioning of the survivors, it transpired that they were laying in ambush for a rival village and hadn't expected the soldiers to be passing. The incident, like many others, never made it back to the British public's awareness.

Sam shook and cleared his head. He had paid homage to Danny's passing on Thursday and would relive the horror, but more importantly celebrate the life and memories of Danny again in twelve months, just as he did for so many others.

Part of the puzzle was why he had supposedly sobered up whilst walking several miles away from his intended destination, the desolate Minera Mountain. And why whisky? He had no memory prior to this, just a vague recollection of climbing the bleak terrain on a seldom trod animal path and then...nothing.

This simple walk across the Mineran landscape had thwarted him several times and, in hindsight, in suspicious circumstances. The first time he had tried to traverse the mountain, he had chosen a route parallel to the commonly used Clywedog Trail. Offset by a mile or so, as Sam preferred solitude, his GPS and phone failed as he got nearer to the mountain. This was nothing uncommon in mountainous areas, and as he progressed even further amongst the rocky outcrops, even his old-fashioned compass started to move erratically. Puzzled, but again not overly concerned as the large iron deposits in the old mining area could account for this, Sam continued on. His ascent became more difficult, more of a climb than a walk and he remembered thinking it certainly wasn't a sheep track anymore, there must be mountain goats around. The next thing he remembered was finding himself sat down by a stream a mile or so to the east, with his water flask in one hand and a half-eaten chocolate bar in the other. His head was feeling foggy, like the onset of a bad cold, and he could not for the life of him remember how he got there. His first fear was that it might be the onset of post-traumatic stress causing blackouts. He had never suffered them before, but he knew some who did.

With hindsight he now realised that he should have been more suspicious, and not doubted his own mental state.

The second time was almost a week later, the day after his friend's wedding, which was the sole reason he was staying in North Wales. It was, in honesty, a mediocre affair at a run-of-the-mill hotel on the outskirts of the town. Nobody had warned the owners that a deluge of current and ex-military would swarm into their abode like a devouring plague of locusts. The food had run out early on and people had had to order out for pizza. Sam had known for a while that he was no longer a big drinker and seeing the pace his old friends and colleagues were setting at the bar, he had instead turned his attentions elsewhere and futilely sought solace with the bridesmaids.

He had woken up alone. A B&B is a lonely place to be after a wedding, waking up with strange scents, or more to the point, smells that were not from the familiar army dormitory. 'God, that sounds so bad', Sam thought as he pushed the chintzy quilt to one side and groaned as his head politely reminded him that humans and alcohol really don't get along with each other. Even a person who liked to be alone with nature, to listen to the call of the wilderness and preferred to be at one with the open sky, can be reminded that sometimes people need more than solitude. His previous life's mistress had been a khaki uniform and he no longer had her. He didn't really have any living family and damned few civilian friends.

Upon feeling the walls of his room enclose upon him, he decided that a bit of Welsh scenery and fresh air would perk him up. He was only stopping in Wales for another week, then it was time to see Matt in Manchester and discuss his offer of becoming an operative in his corporate security firm. Sam wasn't thrilled with the opportunity. Society could afford to lose a few of the rich, pimple-faced executives with cosmetically rebuilt columellae, whose egos led them to believe they were important enough to require protected chauffeuring. Sam pictured it as babysitting inebriated, coke-snorting, philandering asshats. It was a living and it would pay well, boy did it pay well, but was it really what he wanted?

With a maudlin head, he'd set off for Minera Mountain again. On that second attempt, he had woken up at the bottom of a ravine, badly bruised, clothes shredded and he had a sore gash on his head which had by then clotted. He had berated himself for what could only have been his clumsiness, although he could not understand how a twenty-year, surefooted veteran could make such a stupid and what would have been fatal slip in his previous career. He could not account for a couple of hours and was concerned that, whilst he did not feel cold, he must have been unconscious on the ground for a quite a while. A hungover medic from the previous night's wedding festivities reluctantly agreed to call into Sam's B&B. After giving him a quick once-over, and telling Sam not to go walking when still drunk, his prognosis was that his thick skull was normal except it housed a Homer-sized brain.

With only a day left before Tuesday's meeting with Matt, he decided upon one last trip to Minera, to beat that damned mountain.

He didn't like to give in or fail; he always strove to overcome obstacles and he wouldn't give into the inexplicable foreboding that his inner voice was expressing. Why would he be worried about a small Welsh mountain? He'd been in worse mountain ranges and ones where nearly every goat herder held an ageing Kalashnikov. This was possibly the last of his free time before he settled down, the last of the global roaming expeditions and he didn't want it to be marred by one little hummock in Wales. His "walkabouts" had been as much about him finding himself again as it was about discovering the now non-war-torn parts of the world that he had seen as a soldier. Sam felt he needed to revisit some of the towns and villages that he saw from behind the sights of his SA80 or only knew as bombed-out wasteland. Part of him needed to know that they had recovered, that the people had continued regardless of what atrocities that had befallen there. He needed to see there was good in the world and that he himself could move on. Twenty years of army life and the experiences therein had left him with a jaded and sad view of humanity.

The whisky was an obscure Scottish single malt called Glendrumlindeen, aged twenty years and the label declared they were spent in a mix of sherry casks. It was certainly not a brand Sam had heard of before. A quick Google search produced the company website. It displayed a small, family-run Highland distillery which wouldn't have the capacity to sell large amounts wholesale. They did offer an e-commerce section on their website and the questionable bottle was available for a hefty sum of £99.99 excluding postage.

'Jesus, I wish I remembered drinking that', Sam thought as he unscrewed the bottle. He swirled the dregs around the bottom and sniffed as the aroma emanated from the bottle's orifice. 'Dark, moody and a slight hint of burnt wood, I'd say', Sam mused to himself, 'but I'm certainly no connoisseur'.

He'd called in a favour with one of the only army nerds that he knew. Forty-five minutes later he was looking at the previous year's commerce history for the site.

A quick text search via Ctrl and F for the term "Wrexham" brought up only one entry for the surrounding area: a case of 12 bottles that was sent to a residence near Minera twelve weeks ago. Nothing conclusive, but it was certainly worthy of further investigation. Sam typed quickly on the keyboard and brought up a street map and satellite photos of a small hamlet a couple of miles away: the village of Minera. It was a curious mix of domestic and industrial buildings, and from the top-down view what seemed to be a large courtyard fronted by terraced houses filled the screen. The whole hamlet backed onto a sheer cliff, almost as if it was built into an old stone quarry. With only one road in, it wandered around what could only be described as a typical grassy village square. It was certainly large enough for HGVs to drive around as there were two in the satellite photo. There were a lot of cold-looking clouds behind the hamlet. The cliff was high enough to cause an orographic lift, where any warm air was forced upwards into the atmosphere by the obstructing hill, to where it cooled and condensed into clouds. 'Must be cold and damp there', Sam thought. 'That hamlet will be over-shadowed for most of the morning'.

As Sam walked down the worn and creaky staircase, Mrs Williams nosily popped her head out from behind the lounge door. 'Going out, Sam?' she enquired. 'You mind the chill now. It looks warm with that spring sun shining, but once you're in the shade you'll feel it. Mark my words.'

'Thank you, Mrs Williams.' Sam didn't actually know her first name as she always referred to herself and her husband as Mr and Mrs Williams. A newspaper would rustle whenever Mr Williams heard his name, as if to prove his very existence. 'I will keep wrapped up. I might be back late; I have the key.'

'Ok dearie, we'll see you at breakfast. Mr Williams bought some lovely tomato sausage for tomorrow, butcher's best, none of that supermarket rubbish.'

Sam could almost make out the barely discernible mumbled reply from the lounge as he made his way to the front door. 'See you in the morning, have a nice day, Mrs Williams.'

CHAPTER 2

Sam left the B&B, giving the solidly built wooden door a little rattle to make sure it latched. He turned right out of the front garden and ambled off in a north-west direction. Deep in thought, he paced himself as he was in no rush to cover the four or so mile walk to Minera.

To the casual observer, he failed to notice the dirty blue plumber's van with two occupants parked further up the street. However, since Saturday he'd been more alert and silently observed many curious things. He didn't like being toyed with, and it was only with a large effort that he refrained from walking the other way and yanking the passenger out as he passed. As Sherlock would have said: 'The game is afoot'. Sam had no idea what game he was in the middle of, but he would soon.

They didn't need to be close enough to recognise Sam as he left the B&B, they had been watching him and his preparations for departure on the small screen disguised as a TomTom sat nav.

'He's leaving now,' a gruff voice reported into a collar microphone. 'Charcoal jacket, jeans, black boots and a nondescript black peaked cap. I don't know if you were watching, but he's packing.'

'Ok, Phon, if he's coming straight here it should be about an hour. We'll let you know when he arrives. Give it a couple of hours then pick up his belongings and retrieve the cameras. Inform the landlady that he was in an accident and you are there to collect up his personal belongings. You know the drill.'

Xenophon, or Phon to his friends, watched the feed from the drone camera which was parked across the road, slightly north of Sam's B&B in a neighbour's gutter. It was as small as Phon could make it using the commonly available parts, with only a small lens protruding above the rim of the channel. Operational parameters prevented him from using their high-tech gadgets. The low quality and poor battery life of commercially available stuff was a pain, and the sheer bulkiness of the components was certainly a challenge.

'Yeah,' Gruff replied, as he leant over to retrieve his briefcase from behind the passenger seat. 'Do you want to be Jones or Llywelyn?' he asked his partner as he took out two warrant cards along with two faded clip-on ties.

'Llywelyn,' Phon replied, over-emphasising the "Ll" with phlegm and managing not to spit all over Gruff as he mimicked the Welsh accent. 'But let's go for a coffee first, we can't do anything for a while, and we should swap this for the Astra,' he said, tapping the metal of the van with his knuckle.

~*~

The unpaved, poorly maintained tarmac road meandered lazily through the countryside, as if people would have all the time in the world to get to their destination. It was certainly not a Roman military road, Sam thought to himself as he came upon a section that wasn't even wide enough for it to have central dividing white lines. The surrounding fields had a smattering of arable, horticultural and livestock, where small, tired-looking hedges enclosed grassy areas. Only the livestock fields had solid boundaries, which consisted of patched mesh fencing filling in the gaps between sections of hedge.

Sam was, despite the reason for this outing, enjoying the fresh air and open space. It was a little before 11 am, the sun was shining, and a varied selection of birds were singing a plethora of songs trying to attract mates now that spring had arrived. For a backwater road, the traffic was certainly busier than he had anticipated. Heavy diesel fumes from the lorries marred what would have been a most pleasant walk. As Sam rounded a long right-hand bend, he could see the slate roofs and grey stone walls of buildings ahead: journey's end. As he craned his neck a little to see more clearly over the hedges, he failed to notice that the driver of a white pickup gave him more than the customary casual glance as he drove past towards the hamlet.

Walking around a slow, lazy curve of the road, Sam had a better view of the exterior buildings. Two-storey Victorian terraced houses, olde-English style in dull grey stone had pointed gables with intricate carvings on the bargeboards and roof finials. Judging by the size and design of the windows, the buildings were pre-1850s, as the abolishment of the window and brick tax in that year made two-storey houses with bay windows prolific. There were five terraced houses on each side of a double-gated roadway facing the road. As Sam walked closer, he felt the downdraft and then vacuum pull from a passing lorry as it drove as close to Sam and the grass verge as possible to increase its available turning circle for the right-hander into the hamlet. Diesel fumes spewed all around the articulated unit as it changed gear, great black clouds billowing from the twin exhausts mounted vertically behind the cab. Sam paused to let it pass, giving him a few seconds more to study the buildings. There were no signs, street name or company insignia on view. The driver must have been here before to drive so confidently in through the gated entrance.

Sam walked across the road towards the hamlet. The large and sturdy iron gates hung from the side walls of the end terrace houses, each having a small wheel to help support their immense weight. The drop bolt holes in the metalled road contained old and crusty detritus, indicating they hadn't been used recently, although he noted that the stout hinges were rust-free and covered in dark grease.

Walking between the drab stone sides of the houses, Sam could see the access way open up into a large square. Several lorries were parked up by the communal green. He could see their drivers sat in the small greasy spoon café with huge mugs of tea. Old-fashioned doorstop sandwiches filled their hands, and their cheeks bulged like hoarding hamsters. Not wishing to stand out, Sam walked across and entered the café. Instantly the aroma of freshly-ground coffee and smoky bacon assailed his nostrils. Behind the counter was an elderly lady with the air of a hospital matron. She was taking the plates through to the kitchen that a young, pleasant-looking waitress had passed to her. The young waitress was anything but matronly. A brunette, in her early twenties, short black sleeved shirt with the name "Pat" embroidered above her left breast. She wore a short black skirt with a tiny white pinny, and her legs, which were definitely not short, were encased in black hosiery finished with dainty black shoes with a slight heel that gave her calves a defined shape that Sam appreciated.

She glanced across at Sam and pulled a small pad from her pocket on the front of her pinny and made her way towards him.

'Hi, what will it be?' she asked with a smile.

'Black coffee, please. Decaf if you have it.'

'Sure, hun.' She scribbled down his order. 'Anything else? Aunt Mae's Spring Chill Buster breakfast sandwich is popular today. Homemade granary bread, three rashers of local smoky bacon, griddled not fried, field mushrooms, baked white pudding and a griddled flat sausage meat patty. Keep it local and keep it healthy, Aunt Mae always says,' she said, with a smile that flashed her pearly white teeth. She delicately nibbled the end of the pen as she waited for him to answer.

Nice up-sell, Sam thought to himself; no wonder the drivers were piling the food away. Realising that he was peckish after his walk, it would give him an excuse to linger for longer in the café and allow him to observe life outside of the window. 'Ok, you talked me into it.'

After scribbling the order, she tore the top slip of paper from her pad to give to Aunt Mae at the counter. As she spun to walk away, a delicate scent of flowers floated across to Sam. It was an unusual fragrance, reminiscent of the light freshness of a summer meadow. 'Miss, sorry, I couldn't help but notice your unusual perfume, it's quite unique. Could I enquire what it is?'

She looked at him with soft brown eyes, 'I distil the essence from the petals of a local flower,' she said, slightly cocking her head to one side as if studying him. 'It's an old family recipe,' she continued as she walked away.

Sam unashamedly watched her rear as she walked away

only to be caught by the steely gaze of Aunt Mae. Sam turned his head away and stared through the window. A robin with a bright chest landed on the window sill, making short hops along it as if it was trying to find a way in. Curious, he had smelt the fragrance before, but it didn't make sense. He'd smelt it on several occasions in his room at the B&B, as he roused from sleep. Mrs Williams only wore Chanel No. 5, as befitted her generation and she was not one for flowers in the house. The scent was one of the mysteries that had brought him here in a roundabout way. However, why would the scent of a waitress from nowhere be in his room and how could anyone creep up on him in his sleep? Years of sleeping in enemy territory had left him a light sleeper, and it was impossible to navigate Mrs Williams' staircase without making a noise, he'd tried. It wasn't just the centre of the treads that creaked, but even the outer edges where they joined the inner and outer string. He'd even tried gently shinning up the one-inch tops of the strings, but to no avail. The whole staircase was so old and had shrunk with age so that it groaned and wailed like a banshee.

Gazing past the robin, Sam could see the communal green was a grass square, which was approximately fifty metres in size with benches scattered around interwoven pathways, all leading to a large central feature. From this distance, Sam could not make out the details, but it appeared to be a collection of animals. There was a small village shop across the way, with the usual plethora of outside tables displaying crates of vegetables under a faded canopy. Houses surrounded the front section of the square, small offices in the middle and to the rear, a large brick built industrial warehouse with four sets of double doors and an eave height that would comfortably accommodate a double-decker. As Sam studied it, one set of doors opened and the articulated lorry, whose wake had fervently tried to drag Sam into the road earlier, pulled out. The curtain sides were closed, but judging by the bounce of the vehicle it was leaving the warehouse empty. Sam cast a glance at the other articulated vehicles parked along the kerb. All of them had the third axle lifted, indicating empty or very light loads. In a cloud of billowing fumes, the lorry pulled up in front of the others and the rumble of the engine died down. After a few minutes, the driver climbed down from the cab and walked towards the café.

Sam's food arrived with a clatter as the plate and cutlery was slid in front of him. 'I see you've met George.'

Sam looked up at the girl with a puzzled expression.

'The robin.' She indicated with her hand. It was still stood there on the sill; its head cocked looking at them and showing a total disregard for the trucks or the driver walking towards it. 'He's a cheeky little bugger; he'll come right in if you leave the door open.'

As she mentioned the door, the driver walked into a delicate, cascading tinkle of the small brass bell above the door announcing his arrival. He took a seat by the far wall and Sam again unashamedly admired the view as she walked towards the new customer and listened as she greeted him like an old friend.

'The usual, Tony?'

Tony concurred, although his thick Brummie accent made it almost impossible to understand unless you were familiar with Birmingham's dialect and mannerisms.

Pat didn't bother with the pad this time; her aunt nodded across from the counter to confirm she'd heard Tony. Sam realised that Pat was acutely aware that he was watching from behind, and when she stretched herself further over a table than was required to clean the furthest corners, causing her short skirt to ride up the back of her shapely thighs, Aunt Mae's caustic voice rang out in admonishment. 'Enough of that, Apate! And please clear Mark's plates from table two!'

'Apate', not a name he was familiar with and not the Patricia he was expecting. Making a mental note to look it up later, Sam again averted his gaze through the window and for a split second thought George was giving him an objurgating stare, before merrily hopping away.

He tuned out the chatter and kitchen noises as he studied the buildings outside. One of the occupants of those houses had probably ordered the Glendrumlindeen, an expensive vice for someone who lived in a terrace house in the back end of nowhere. Obviously, there was no way to snoop around those premises today; besides the drivers and himself, there were very few people around. There was occasionally a handful of warehouse staff milling around between deliveries and a gardener attending the flower beds on the green. Sam was aware that he would be conspicuous if he loitered for no good reason. The only building of interest was the warehouse, which ironically was a visually unimpressive structure. Something wasn't right with this place, and he couldn't put his finger on it. It wasn't unusual to have Victorian industrial buildings with the workers' dwellings nearby, but they weren't normally part of the same gated community.

The houses were impeccably maintained, as were the yards and gardens. The shop looked worn and tired but besides the faded canopy it was pristine; the windows were clean and the woodwork showed no sign of rot or neglect. Looking around the café, Sam noticed the floor had a deep shine like it was polished on a regular basis, not just cleaned. The drivers seemed oblivious to all of this; their banter was about traffic, roadworks, today's Page Three model and the usual mundane small talk of tired and weary males. The original group had finished their food, paid and left, taking their trucks with them. A continual cycle of transporters cycled through the hamlet. Every twenty minutes a new truck would arrive – it was a smooth and well thought-out logistical process. Three trucks every hour would pull in, enter the warehouse via one of three sets of double doors and exit empty out of the fourth door ready to park up. All had pulled up for at least a forty-five minute rest. That duration meant that they had had quite a drive before or ahead of them. The tachograph recorded the driver's times which ensured they stuck to the law regarding rest stops every four and a half hours of driving. Whatever they were delivering, it wasn't local.

Sam finished his second coffee and pushed the plate and mug into the centre of the table. He was glad he hadn't gone for the full-caff now. He didn't want his hands getting the caffeine shakes later. Rising, he asked Pat if he could have the bill and paid a visit to the gents'. It didn't surprise him to find that the toilets were spotless and smelt fresh. Mentally he always gauged the kitchen cleanliness by the condition of the toilets. The unmistakable sound of the Dyson hand drier would have given Pat a twelve-second heads-up on Sam's exit time. The incredibly cheap bill for £4.25 was on the table upon his return. He tipped the change from a fiver and walked out, having complimented Mae and Pat on the excellent food.

Walking towards the green, he feigned interest in the sculpture, keeping to one of the paths supplied and mindful of the "keep off the grass" signs. Noticing the questioning look from the gardener he commented, 'The sculpture intrigued me, I just had to have a look before I left.'

The detail and finesse of the bronze sculpture surprised Sam, as did the size. At 8 feet in diameter and almost the same in height, it depicted a nature scene with nearly every local insect, plant and animal Sam could think of, from the lowly earthworm at the roots of a small crop of wheat, a ladybird and a bee on a raspberry, to a hawk and an owl perched on opposite sides an old apple tree. It was, to him, a symbolic cross-section of UK nature and wildlife, a snapshot of how beautiful the countryside was if you took the time to look.

For a few minutes, he forgot the reason for coming so close to the warehouse as he studied the feature before him. He half expected the mice to run away and the blackbirds or frogs to eat the odonates, such was the quality and craftsmanship.

'Breathtaking, isn't it? I find it a reliable way to gauge the nature of a man. Those that fail to behold its beauty and hopefully ruminate about nature's decline due to the onset of mankind, well, they tend to have little or no morality in my experience,' said the patronising old man.

'It's certainly finely crafted,' replied Sam, turning towards the gardener. He was an old man, a worn and sinewy person, like a piece of rawhide left out in the sun for too long. Tired-looking, but there was intelligence there. Sam could see an alertness in those eyes.

'We are very proud of it; it symbolises what we believe in around here. Working together, joined with nature, symbiotically, not as a parasite bleeding its host.'

'That sounds a little cultish,' Sam interjected.

'No, not at all, we are just a group of locals who collaborate for mutual benefit. Just like any other village or farming community around here.' The old man looked up from the flower bed. Sam recognised the flowers, but not having any personal interest in gardening, he didn't know their names. 'We don't get many visitors here, only the drivers and they're not interested in much. They're happy enough as long as the coffee is hot, and the bacon is thick, besides that there's not much to see this far from the main road. I take it you will be heading back soon. I noticed you didn't arrive in a car, that road can be dangerous for pedestrians. I can ask one of the drivers if they will give you a lift if you want.'

Realising he was not going to get any further unimpeded reconnaissance of the warehouses, Sam decided to withdraw. 'I'm OK thanks, but I suppose I should head back to town, it was nice speaking with you. The garden is lovely, very calming.' Sam turned and slowly walked across the green to the shop.

After a few minutes browsing along each aisle, he picked up a packet of sugar-free gum and a small pack of handy wipes. The shop was unremarkable in the way of produce variety, except there was no children's paraphernalia, sweets or comics and it was heavily into fresh produce. It didn't feel like a village shop, either, it felt familiar, structured, and orderly. Placing his items at the till, he asked the assistant, 'Do you have any bottles of Glendrumlindeen?'

'I'm afraid not sir, sorry, we have an exceptional fifteen-year-old single malt at the back. Glendrumlindeen is a lovely smooth whisky, but it's a little pricey for most of my customers,' the elderly cashier replied. 'That'll be £3.53 please.'

'So you have heard of it?' Sam enquired as he paid, noting the strong, calloused hands on the old man. Not the typical hands of a shopkeeper, those were from hard labour -- and a lifetime of it.

'Don't mind my hands, sir, I grow all the vegetable you see here. We're very independent around here, self-sufficient you might say,' he explained as he saw Sam looking at his hands. 'And yes, I enjoy a tipple or two of Glendrumlindeen now and again; as I said it's a smooth malt, as the name suggests, from a glacial valley in Aberdeenshire.' He handed the change to Sam, who promptly deposited it into the "Save the Rainforest" charity tin. Having a pocket full of jingly coins was definitely not desirable at that moment.

With no reason to walk back into the compound, and with the staff near the warehouse staring in Sam's direction, he made his way back to the road. 'I need to get in there', he thought to himself and set off formulating a plan.

CHAPTER 3

As Sam drew parallel to the gates, he realised that he had only observed the trucks arriving from the west, coming from the A525. The roadway to the east looked as if it had infrequent use as the branches of the trees encroached on the head space required by an articulated trailer. Sam considered wandering up there to see if there was another way in, but remembering the satellite photos, thought better of it.

It took him five minutes to come upon one of the few long straight stretches on the road, luckily this one had what he required. An articulated lorry had passed him a few minutes ago and thanks to the tortuous, almost convoluted road, he should be able to see the top of the next curtain-sided trailer minutes before it got to his location.

The farmer's gate was typical of most, in that the only form of locking mechanism was a simple drop latch. A handful of sheep were lovingly eyeing up the tall grass that grew between the tractor tracks leading up to the gate. Their field had been shorn low by the multitude of fellow sheep grazing there. One budding escapologist was squeezing its head under the gate via the tyre depression. Upon hearing Sam approach, it struggled to break free, leaving a few tufts of wool on the bottom of the gate. Sam opened the tubular steel gate and let it swing until it caught in the long grass as if a farmer had merely failed to latch it correctly. This left a small opening for sheep to exit one at a time. Making his way further along the road, he located a hole in the hedge of an arable field, large enough for him to squeeze through. Acres of three-foot tall sprout plants spread out in front of him, most of which had been picked clean by the farm labourers at some point over the winter, starting from the bottom of the stem where the sprouts bulked out first and maybe revisiting them in a few weeks to pick the top section. Thanks to a childhood vacation on an aunt's farm, Sam knew that hand picking was tough on the fingers and damned cold in the winter frost. He was surprised to see that some farmers had resisted modernisation; a sprout harvester would have cut the each stem at the ground and fed it through the de-leafer, stripping the sprouts from the stem as it did so and then ejecting it back on the ground. God, he hated sprouts, foul tasting things.

Having assured himself that there were no farm workers in the field, he crouched and waited for the next truck. Within 10 minutes he heard the roar of the engine as it drove around the bend onto the long straight. Three sheep had wandered across the road to graze on the long tender grass of the verge. Sam heard the vehicle slow down and then crawl towards the sheep. As it passed, he caught a glimpse of a miserable looking driver as he honked his horn. The sheep took little notice, having heard the trucks roar by all of their lives. With a squeal of brakes, the truck came to a slow stop, and the driver begrudgingly exited the cab to shoo the daft animals out of the way.

Sam watched as the driver walked around the front of the cab. Sam stealthily crept from his hiding place and snuck under the trailer's under-ride guard beneath the trailer bed. Not having hidden under a lorry before he was not really sure what to expect, but he knew border patrols and customs officials regularly removed would-be immigrants from articulated axles. Thankfully, the weather was dry and so was the underside of the trailer. Cramped and perilously balanced on an axle between two bulbous air reservoirs for the braking system, Sam held on to the cross-beams while waiting for his unwitting chauffeur to move off.

He had previously thought that being in the back of the army's eight-tonne trucks was the world's worst ride, but now he knew differently. Sam would never have dreamt the journey of a quarter of a mile could possibly be as nerve-wracking as this. He was, of course, bereft of the truck's suspension. He felt every bump, stone and pothole all the way up to his teeth. The road seemed to zoom along at a hundred miles an hour, even though he knew the lorry was only doing a maximum of forty. Every twist of the road threatened to dismount him from his precarious perch, which would result in him either being run over, squashed between the axle and road or worse, dragged alive while the tarmac stripped away his flesh. The dust billowed up from the road, threatening to deposit grit into Sam's scrunched-up eyes. To breathe, he had to cover his mouth and nose with the crook of his arm while still maintaining a firm hold on the chassis. The thirty-second trip was more of a sphincter-clenching, white-knuckle ride than anything he had ridden in the theme parks and thankfully the deafening screech from the brakes signalled the end of the nightmare. Below him, he saw the painted tarmac of the warehouse floor and to his vast relief, it was stationary. The steady vibrations of the idling engine continued to rattle his teeth and make his pectoral muscles jiggle up and down. He smiled to himself as he thought, 'I'm armed, hanging for dear life under a truck, trying to break into God knows what and I am worried about jogger's nipple'.

The conscientious driver, wanting to allow the turbo to cool down correctly to prolong its life, let the engine idle for a few minutes. Eventually, to Sam's relief, the jiggling stopped, silence surrounded him like a blanket of bliss and every muscle screamed out in protest.

The driver exited the cab after a few seconds and proceeded to uncouple the clasps holding the curtain on his side of the trailer. Sam heard the whirr of an electric forklift as it drove around the front to park alongside where Sam was still hunched. It was quickly followed by a second. The ratchet catch at the back of the trailer clicked as the tension was removed. The forklift driver lifted the front bar, which then allowed the curtain side to be pulled to the rear. Sam only had a few seconds to make his escape before the driver repeated the process on the near side of the truck.

He silently lowered himself to the ground. A quick scan for personnel and cameras showed only three cameras, all of which were pointing toward the entrances. The warehouse was a large, open-plan design. It had four sets of closed double doors, each set leading to a burgundy painted roadway. This gave the lorry drivers a clear indication where they should drive. Each had a large rectangle for the designated loading bay. The 30-foot span between the painted roadways was separated by low pseudo walls created by various crates and stacks of blue

GKN pallets. With few precious seconds left, Sam rolled beneath the under-ride, crouched and quickly made his way to a collection of stacked crates.

Sam heard one of the forklifts as it approached from the rear of the trailer and the clatter of the tines echoed across the semi-deserted warehouse as it set the pallet down near his hiding place. A quick flash of red and it was trundling around the cab as the other appeared from the rear. The lorry driver walked around and started unfastening the clasps on this side. As he pulled the curtain side back, Sam had his first glance at the cargo: thirteen blue pallets per side, each containing four nondescript black, fifty-five-gallon metal drums. The forklift drove away as it deposited the fourth pallet. He could see a small label on each barrel, but it was too far away to read. Keeping his head well below the level of the barrels, he made his way out from between the crates towards the barrels, crouching down just as a forklift delivered the fifth pallet.

In the dim light, Sam could just about read the label. Each drum was identical, and each stated that the contents were Liqualin CC, a highly alkaline industrial cleaning agent suitable for the food industry.

'FFS, this can't be right', Sam thought as he crept back to the safety of the crates. He was sure something nefarious must have been happening, none of this made sense. He almost stood up and walked out. What would they say? 'Hey you! You shouldn't be here, get out.' He'd risked life and limb under the lorry for nothing and generally made a fool out of himself.

He steeled himself as his gut instinct told him that he should look around a little bit more, as his gut had served him well in the past. The artic was efficiently unloaded, and the driver drove along the burgundy track and out of the fourth doorway. The solid looking doors swung open automatically for him and closed afterwards, returning the interior to a yellowy incandescent gloom.

One of the forklifts was moving around the wall furthest from the doors. It picked up and removed an extra-wide stack of crates -- the speed at which this was performed suggested that the boxes were not as loose and haphazardly-stacked as their appearance suggested. The removal revealed a grey, metal-framed exit, leading on to a wide rubber conveyor belt. The belt went up into the darkness on a trajectory that would take it through the back wall, just below the eaves. Three more electric forklifts appeared from behind the rear pallets, each with powerful floodlights mounted on the top of the safety cab. Sam ducked down, the shadows of his hiding place swaying in front of him as the trucks manoeuvred close by. He heard a hard clang of metal on metal as the tines jangled on the carriage. The shadows moved violently and suddenly he was back in the gloom as the trucks raced the short distance toward the conveyor. Peeking around the crates, Sam could just make out that unlike the other forklifts, these had specific drum carrying attachments. The lead truck rotated its drum, various hydraulic pipes becoming taut with the pressurised fluid that controlled the hydraulic rams. It carefully deposited the drum on the metal framework, where it gently rolled towards the end of the conveyor. As the area was now illuminated by the trucks' lights, Sam could clearly see the conveyor. It had large lugs which were spaced at regular intervals along the rubber belt, preventing the barrels from rolling back as they were quickly transported into the murky shadows above. Within ten minutes, 104 barrels disappeared as the forklifts whisked about in a precisely choreographed dance. All the pallets were stacked away, the opening was covered again, and the warehouse returned to a yellow crepuscular glow provided by the underpowered ceiling mounted bulbs.

Now that was unusual, he thought, peering from behind his cover to look up into the darkness.

No sooner had the lights gone out than the double doors opened once again. Sam realised that his little escapade with the sheep had cut their timing to the bone. The process repeated itself, only, this time, there was a few minutes to spare between each delivery.

As Sam was stuck there all day, he realised that it was only because the adapted barrel-carrying forklifts were so well obscured that they had prevented their drivers from seeing his crouched run from the artic earlier. As Sam watched from the relative safety provided by the crates, he used the wet wipes to clean away the grime from his under-truck voyage. At approximately four-thirty the last delivery arrived. Upon completion of their task, the workmen called it a day, parked their trucks at the charging stations, locked up the front doors and disappeared through an unseen door that Sam heard close, but could not see.

Pausing to listen for any stragglers, he jogged towards the hidden conveyor. Sam squeezed past the crates, jumped and continued to jog up the now-still rubber into the darkness. He could feel the air change as he passed through the side of the building into what he could only assume was a cavern, cave or tunnel into the rock face. His shadows caused by the warehouse lights danced onto the rubber, obscuring the lugs and making progress dangerous. He paused; there was a faint glow ahead, possibly a hundred feet or so, but not enough to proceed safely. Taking his pocket torch out, he shielded the beam with his hand and clicked through the brightness settings with the rubber toggle on the bottom. With the torch set on low and wishing he had brought the red filter to preserve his night vision, he continued upwards.

As he progressed higher, he could hear rhythmic clanks of automated machinery and slowly it came into view. The barrels were corralled onto a series of metal holding frames. A robotic arm hung expectantly at the end of the conveyor waiting to grasp any barrel that nudged its sensors and placed it on to the gravity-fed racks. Sam did a quick count and calculated that there were nearly a thousand barrels still in the stands. At the end of the colossal framework, a barrel would move out onto a set of rollers that caused it to rotate and spin around like an energetic break-dancer while a pair of nozzles sprayed it with a clear liquid. Counting the seconds, each barrel was thoroughly sprayed every twenty seconds with a few seconds for the liquid to set and then it was rolled off into the darkness again. Three lorries per hour, eight hours a day, 104 drums each, nearly two and a half thousand barrels a day.

'A mighty strange operation for barrels of a commercial cleaner', Sam muttered to himself.

He lowered himself to an inspection gantry and followed it 'round as it took him closer to the spraying apparatus. His access was blocked by a latched gate and warning sign proclaiming the fumes from the spray to be hazardous if inhaled. He looked across and saw a large extractor funnel presumably removing the noxious vapours.

He saw another gantry butted up against the rock face, with large domed wall lights providing enough light for him to stow his torch. The walkway followed the next conveyor down another dimly lit tunnel. The dry walls had machine marks which clearly indicated that it was man-made and not a natural occurrence. There were several steel doors on the side of the tunnel, securely locked with no visible latch or locking mechanism on this side. Sam came upon a row of twelve lockers, each one held a garment that he recognised with trepidation. He'd had to wear, train and fight in enough versions of a CBRN suit to recognise these. Chemical, biological, radiological and nuclear protective suits, or Hazmats if you were a civilian. These were top of the range. Each had a self-contained breathing apparatus to ensure a supply of breathable air and had a variety of dosimeters and detection patches on the arms.

Sam took a step back from the locker, looked at a barrel which was trundling past and looked back at the meters on the arms.

'Oh shit!' he involuntarily expelled, as he checked every locker. Each was a duplicate of the first. He examined the detector patches to check their status, each was thankfully clear. Upon noticing a portable Geiger counter at the base of a locker, he turned it on.

There was no audible clicking, just a large display with quantified radiation levels displayed. Each level was stylised with an icon and with an indicative colour signifying the threat level. Thankfully the needle was in the safe zone, and Sam placed the device back and closed all of the doors.

All that shit about keeping it fresh and local when they're dumping toxic waste down the mines. Sam removed his iPhone from his jacket. Obviously, there was no signal underground. He typed a detailed message to Matt. This was pretty serious, and he needed to get the word out to the authorities. If he was unfortunate and something happened to him, the perpetrator would more than likely remove any items he carried to examine later.

If they took the phone above ground, it would reconnect and send the message. Let the full force of the law fall upon you. Next, he took a few photos as evidence and attached them to a second email to Matt.

Sam continued to look along the tunnel and found a few more doors further down. One led to a tiled room, with aggressive looking full-body shower arrays. Another was a toilet block which he gratefully used, though he dared not flush because of the noise.

The last door before the gantry terminated held a frosted mesh window. Fluorescent light shone through from the room behind. Creeping up to it, Sam carefully listened for any activity and scanned the door for any locks or alarms. Curiously it had neither, just an old-fashioned heavily-worn brass door knob. Slowly opening the door a fraction to peer through, Sam saw a corridor going left and right. From the crack he had created between the door and jamb he could just make out a corner at the far end where the corridor angle hit the toilet block. Opening the door silently, he stepped into the frame to allow his left eye to peek the other way. It was clear. There was a set of two blue fire doors thirty feet away; the corridor was illuminated via standard fluorescents, and there was a fire hose on one wall but no cameras. He stepped through and cautiously started to make his way to the fire doors.

Halfway down the corridor, a slight glint of light caught his eye just as he walked into what looked like fine spider threads hanging from the ceiling.

Pain and full-body cramps surged through his body; part of his mind was semi-aware that he had risen onto his tiptoes as all of his muscles were being over-stimulated by the surge of electricity. Arms drawn in towards his body, his shoulders were hunching so much it seemed like his head was trying to retreat, tortoise-like, into his body.

It appeared to go on for an eternity and then suddenly it stopped, and Sam instantly crashed to the floor, gasping for breath, in agony and feeling an unbelievable amount of fatigue. He had previously been hit by Tasers and stun guns as part of his training, but this was more powerful, more aggressive and it pissed him off. He willed his body to stand up, he even saw it in his mind, but when Sam opened one eye, he saw his nose being squashed on the cold quartz epoxy resin floor. His back felt like it had been beaten with a wooden four by four for hours.

Past his nose, he could make out polished black boots, many of them surrounding him, as strong hands lifted him and his head rolled around as if he were an understuffed ragdoll.

'Welcome back, Mr Shepard,' one said as they removed his coat and stripped him there in the corridor. He was powerless to resist. 'I'm glad you managed not to defecate yourself, although using the firehose on you would have been amusing.'

They plastic-cuffed his hands tightly behind his back and limply frogmarched him butt naked and barefooted through the doors. Sam lost his sense of direction and the distance that they half dragged, half carried him. His mind wasn't working clearly yet, but he was also glad that he had used the toilet before exiting through the door.

CHAPTER 4

His face was suddenly pushed into a stout wooden door. Two pairs of firm hands held him there as the plastic cuffs were removed with an accompanying snip. His nose was sending urgent signals to his brain that it had suffered enough today and to please refrain from any further damage. He felt the vibration of the door being unlocked. As soon as the catch was released, the pressure that was holding him to the door catapulted him through the now open doorway, stumbling across the room and collapsing onto a strategically placed wooden bed with a bare mattress. The door slammed shut with a resounding bang. The sound reverberated in Sam's head as he rushed over to a toilet that he hadn't consciously noticed, and vomited.

As he slowly recovered from the Tasering, he started to examine the windowless room. It was a stereotypical prison cell with a small wooden bunk, functional steel toilet with sink on the cistern and a small steel mirror on the wall. The walls were of brick construction with no gaps in the mortar, and they looked well-maintained.

They were painted orange, and the paint looked thick from years of re-coats. He could see two grooves where the bed frame had caught the wall as people were thrown onto it. The grooves showed layers of varying shades of orange, indicating it had probably been a cell for a long time. The floor was the same quartz epoxy that he had noticed before, only orange in colour. This was not a room designed to relax in. There was an ominous floor drain in the far corner. Sam inspected it and tried, unsuccessfully, to prise the small cover loose. A drain in the floor was not normally a good sign in this scenario. Thankfully there was no indication that it had recently been used to wash away any blood.

As his senses came back, Sam saw a pair of bright yellow coveralls that had been knocked off the bed as he had stumbled in; the bright colour making them stand out from between the bed and the wall. Recovering the yellow cotton garment, he found matching socks and a pair of flip-flops. It would be difficult for a prisoner to run or fight in flip-flops.

Having dressed, Sam checked the door. He remembered it being wood from the outside. On the inside, it was covered with a piece of orange painted steel, with an observation hatch at head height which was shuttered on the outside. The door made no movement as Sam put his weight against it and the screen was similarly secure. The toilet was designed with security in mind. It would probably trap his waste further down the line for inspection.

He was just about to check the bed for a loose slat or a high tensile spring with which to make an impromptu weapon, when a disembodied voice from above said, 'I see you found my clue, Sam.'

Sam looked up. There must be a speaker hidden in the

light fitting, he thought. He couldn't reach it for further examination.

'Cat got your tongue, Sam? You weren't this quiet last time you were here.' The poor quality of the speaker removed some of the tonal inflection from the voice. 'Oh yes, you have been here before, although you suspect this already. Go ahead and leave your mark. Your others are there.'

Sam looked at the bed. Whenever he was in a cell, he would always try to leave himself a sign that he had been there before. Disorientation against a prisoner was a powerful tool. Similar cells, different locations, sometimes never knowing where you were because you'd blacked out or been drugged. He looked under the bed at the wooden leg where it met the frame. There were three snake-like grooves scratched into the wood, Sam's S. He looked around to see what he could have used. The only item available was the metal pull tab on the coverall zipper. He removed the garment and etched a fourth S.

'Don't worry about that, Sam, one way or another you will not be coming back here again.'

'Is that a threat?' Sam said, looking up at the ceiling, wondering if they had a camera there as well.

'I am watching you. It must be cold in there,' he chuckled. 'And no, it is not a threat, just a simple statement.'

Sam looked down. 'Funny,' he replied, as he put his legs back into the overalls. Struggling with his arms and broad chest, he finally zipped himself back up.

'You found my clue? Or should I say clues.'

'The whisky?'

'Obviously.'

'Clearly it was a breadcrumb leading somewhere. I didn't expect it to result in a setup like this. Why don't I remember being here?'

'In time, Sam, first tell me what you think you have discovered.'

'The barrels I followed presumably contain toxic waste, and I assume you are dumping them in the mountain. But if that's the case why didn't you kill me last time instead of playing with me?' Sam spat back.

'Speaking of bread, aren't you glad I asked Apate to make sure you had a hearty meal before you left the café? It was a long day after all.'

Sam looked up at the light, pupils dilating not so much from the light as from irritation.

'Did you recognise her perfume at the café? She spent a lot of time in your room while you slept, you know. Studying you, you might say. Oh, and as a precaution, I requested that she file down your firing pins.'

Sam looked up angrily.

'The security on your cases, while being cutting edge on the consumer market, is pretty weak at our level, Sam. Don't look so surprised.'

He sat on the bed, looking slightly up towards the source of the voice, though not at the light to avoid temporary loss of sight.

'Anyway, you have it wrong, Sam. It will all become clear, I promise. This is all part of an audition, or as you would call it, a job interview. We are testing your abilities, Sam. You have done very well so far, but you still have a long way to go. I suggest you answer my questions and play along. We have a lot to do and only a small window of opportunity.'

Sam was getting a stiff neck and feeling foolish looking up while listening. 'How did you find the cameras, Sam? I read the report from the surveillance team. Oh, they have also picked up your personal items from the B&B, I hope you don't mind. Mrs Williams was sorry to hear that you had been in a serious accident and that you would not be returning.'

'If you've hurt her, God help you, I'll –' Sam was cut off.

'Nothing of the sort Sam, she was very obliging. She even made them a cup of tea and a bacon butty each, anything for the boys in blue, she said.'

Sam could hear faint background noises behind the voice, a keyboard and a chair creaking. The quality of the microphone was far greater than the speaker in the cell.

'Apparently you marked three out of four cameras with a section symbol §. A double S, as it were, for Sam Shepard. They were not impressed; you have made them look bad. How did you find them?'

'Tell your crew they are nothing but amateurs. I spotted the sequence of vans and cars parked after my third attempt at Minera. Apate's perfume indicated someone had been in my room. The cameras themselves were easy to find. Few people closely watch a black surveillance screen at night and Mrs Williams' guest room was very dark, thanks to the blackout curtains. Ten seconds with a torch and two bits of transparent red plastic was all it took. Google it, you'll get there!' He said with vehemence in his voice. He was tiring of this charade now. 'How did you get into my room without waking me?'

'Let's just say no one in that house would have woken up even if we marched a herd of elephants up those creaky stairs.'

'You drugged us? How?'

'No, nothing so crude or invasive as that, Sam. You won't believe me at this point in time, but we are not the bad guys.'

'How then?' replied Sam, realising his stoic patience was wearing thin.

'You'll find out if you pass, Sam. You have much to accomplish in the next twenty-four hours. Now tell me, what did you do to the surveillance car and how did you manage it? They made quite a scene driving back into the courtyard this afternoon.' Sam could clearly hear a hint of amusement from the tinny speaker.

'Mrs Williams' grandson, Billy. For the price of an Xbox game, he happily agreed to sabotage the first vehicle that called to the B&B after I left. He was to put a handful of marbles into the exhaust and then to smear the back box with axle grease. Schoolboy stuff. I was just letting you know that I knew I was being toyed with.'

Laughter rang out over the speaker, 'Well played, Sam – although Phon doesn't think so. I'd try and avoid him for a while if I were you.'

Ignoring the humour in the lopsided conversation, Sam enquired, 'So where do we go from here?'

'Where indeed. You have two choices, Sam. Either you do nothing, and you will be shortly escorted to the medical bay. There you will be drugged to induce a substantial memory loss – and I mean large this time. You will wake up in a hospital bed with whatever injuries the guards inflict to make the accident that we informed Mrs Williams about seem real. You won't remember the wedding, Sam, you might not even remember leaving the army last year.' The disembodied voice droned on. 'Or, as your sponsor I wish you to continue with the audition, follow the trail, find out the truth and eventually you will want to work alongside me.'

'And if I don't?'

'If you make it that far Sam, and decide not to join, I will guarantee your safety and release.'

'And what do you want me to do next? Dance like a monkey?'

'Escape! The guards will be here for you soon. Two guards, robust but not the brightest. You need to overpower them and make your way down the corridor. There you will find all of your belongings, including your weapons. There is also a nice warm jumper, I suggest you take it, it's a lot colder out there than you think. Oh, Sam, there is no phone reception where you are going, but I did take the liberty of deleting your phone before it could send your messages. You will need to exit the building via the fire door further along from your possessions and make your way to the base of the mountain. It's nearly six now, so you should make it there for breakfast time.'

'Now I know you're lying. Minera isn't even that big, you can walk right across it in an hour. I will escape and I am going to bring you down, you scum!'

'As I was saying, exit, via the fire door; at the base of the mountain there is a derelict farmstead, I will meet you there. I have taken the liberty of providing a small map and Aunt Mae has made you a few sandwiches to keep your strength up. Good luck Sam, don't fail me.'

The speaker gave an audible click as the line was turned off.

Sam could faintly hear the guards talking as they approached. The clop of their boots were ringing out on the hard surface. He quickly removed his flip-flops and socks, stuffing them under the bed out of sight.

Sam was no novice at hand-to-hand combat but held neither belt nor award in any of the martial arts. He had trained relentlessly with every instructor the army threw at him, and many they hadn't. He had personally combined the qualities and moves from each discipline to a fighting style that suited his body shape. He didn't fight fair, clean, or with honour. He'd been trained to win ruthlessly by any means necessary, but to be an honourable winner once the enemy was safely incapacitated.

He sat on the bed, head in his hands trying to look broken, forlorn and weak. The hatch of the door noisily dropped open with a clang, causing Sam to look up. Hard eyes stared through as Sam, seemingly dejectedly, placed his head back into his hands. As the thud of the heavy wooden hatch slammed shut, Sam sprang to the side of the door. As it slowly opened, he saw a hand on the handle above the overly large old-fashioned mortise key. Sam grabbed the arm, twisted, and threw the assailant into the room. In a quick dash, he whipped through the opening, grabbing the handle and key to slam and lock the door, shutting the guard inside. With one fluid-like action, he had evened the odds.

One down and one to go, he thought. He sprang backwards on both feet like a startled mountain goat, as he sensed, rather than saw, a huge club-like fist swing in a roundabout action towards his face. 'I'm looking forward to this,' The guard drawled. 'After the trouble, you caused the last time. I'm the one who cracked your thick skull. Not that you remember, but that's what you get for kicking a guy in the family jewels.' He knocked on his private area with a dull thud. 'Cup,' he said. 'You'll not get me that way again, you little shit. I don't care what Reb said, I'm gonna hurt you this time. You are, after all, meant to be found broken in an accident.' A cruel grin spread across his face.

Another quick punch flew towards Sam followed by a couple of jabs. He swatted them aside, deflecting the brute force to one side. This guy was strong, ox strong, thought Sam. He was a fist guy, the first rule Sam learnt from his first fighting mentor was that you never box with a boxer. Swatting a few more jabs to one side, Sam waited for the killing shot. He didn't wait long. The brute pulled his shoulder back a fraction too much. He had a tell! A fraction of a second's heads-up before knucklegeddon. Sam side-stepped as it approached. The brute was too big to throw, hold or play with. A quick throw kick to the inside of the brute's far knee shattered it with an audible crack, which was only drowned out by the brute's cry of anguish and expletives. Sam quickly followed it up with a spinning back kick to the head, knocking the lummox out cold.

Sam charitably checked for a pulse and tilted the brute's head to one side to prevent him from choking if he was sick. Ignoring the rants and threats coming from behind the wooden door, Sam removed the key, planning to toss it later. That'll slow them down.

Jogging silently down the corridor in bare feet, he set off to find his equipment. Sam felt strangely good. He missed the adrenalin rush and the thrill and the chase, even if he was the one being chased this time. He realised the quiet life didn't fit well on his shoulders. His walkabouts had quelled the doubts that had haunted his past. He had put those ghosts to rest, and as perverse as it sounded, he was enjoying himself.

CHAPTER 5

He found his clothes and accessories a few turns of the corridor away. The shirt, trousers and jacket hung on a wooden hanger from a door frame, the rest were on a small table. Surprisingly the clothes had been cleaned, dried and ironed. Quickly dressing, Sam finished off by checking his inventory. True to Reb's word, the phone had no signal and the messages and photos had been deleted. The gun was on the table, unloaded and files stripped. He filled the magazines and then assembled the gun, noting that the firing pin had been replaced. Both knives were still in the cuff pockets, and the Iain Sinclair Cardsharp was in his wallet. Mae's sandwiches were wrapped in a brown paper bag, sitting on top of a small rucksack alongside a bottle of Welsh mineral water, a woolly hat and the promised jumper. He stowed the new items in the sack and slung it over his shoulder.

Sam had no inclination to follow Reb's planned route, he just wanted to get out. He needed to get back to the hamlet square, find a phone signal and alert the authorities. As he progressed back up the corridor heading towards the cell, he could hear the sound of alarmed shouts and the rhythmic drum of boots running in his direction.

'Damn it!' he muttered, turning around. 'Ok Reb, we'll try it your way for now.' Sam followed the fire exit signs, looking for the way out. It took several minutes to find the exit as the building he was in was bigger than he expected. He'd passed several side corridors, a few storage rooms and a communal rest area, stocked with fridges and refreshments. He stopped briefly to fill up his bag.

'This is a frickin' warren,' he muttered to himself as he jogged past yet another corridor.

He could still hear the sound of footsteps in the distance, accompanied by doors slamming against walls as the search party performed a methodical room-by-room search.

Finally, he located the door. A solid affair, plain grey and festooned with emergency symbols. Sam put his hand on the crossbar to force the door open and paused. There was a sensor and if he opened it the fire alarm would go off and give away his location. A quick inspection showed it to be a cheap magnetic reed sensor, standard in most office and home security systems. It comprised of two parts: a flat magnet screwed to the door and a small white rectangle screwed to the door frame containing a glass tube with two thin metal reeds. The reeds were millimetres apart unless they were in close proximity to a magnet, then the reeds touched and formed an electrical circuit. No magnet, no circuit and the alarm went off, very easy to fool if you had a magnet.

Sam considered rushing back to the kitchen area as there was a collection of novelty magnets on the fridge. Alas, the banging of the doors was drawing nearer. He pulled one of his thin cuff knives out and jabbed it behind the magnetic plate screwed to the door. Being designed to raise the alarm from intruders from the outside, the small screws were vulnerable from the inside.

A small amount of leverage loosened the screws. Sam had to carefully pry the magnet off the door while maintaining contact with its counterpart. He slowly opened the door, firmly pressing the magnetic bar to the sensor with the blade. He slowly pulled the knife away; the bar stayed in place. But now the screws were the problem, they would catch on the door as he closed it, dislodging the magnet. With the sounds of banging doors drawing closer, he wiggled the strip slightly one way then the other as he removed the screws. He stepped through and carefully closed the door, trying to reduce the noise as the locking mechanism clicked into place.

Outside was colder and darker than he expected. Above the door, a single bulb gave off a dim glow which illuminated a small circle onto the concrete path. Sam cast a quick glance all around. He'd exited from a structure built into the rock. The door opened into a narrow rock fissure with no clear view of the sky above and a concrete path lead the way into the gloom. Turning around, Sam saw that there were no windows in the narrow strip of visible brick. Sam replaced the dagger into his cuff holster and jogged off into the darkness, his dark clothing soon merging with the shadows.

Expecting to emerge from the crevice a few hundred yards behind the hamlet's cliff face, Sam stopped and stared across a vast flat expanse of hedged fields, poorly illuminated by a pale rosy sun descending for sunset. Fields full of livestock or crops created an idyllic shadow filled scene that any true artist would lovingly try to capture.

But where the hell was he? He hadn't thought he'd passed out while being Tasered and if he had it certainly wasn't long enough for him to be moved far. This certainly wasn't Minera and from this side of the hamlet he should be able to see Llandegla in the distance. All he could see was a dirty great big mountain in the distance, fields and lights from a dozen or more clusters of dwellings and small villages that were shadowed by the mountain. He looked up, the sun was in the correct position, but much paler and not as warm as it should be, even for a March sunset.

He looked in the bag and found the map Reb had mentioned. It was roughly drawn on the back of a café napkin. A simple scrolling blue line was drawn from the letter 'A' to 'B'. 'A' was by a drawing of a door and 'B' sat next to a house with a broken roof. Scattered around the napkin were the words 'village'. The mountain was at the top of the next drawing of a derelict house with the words 'Not Mordor'. Sam might have laughed if the situation was not so bewildering.

After a rough calculation, Sam decided he had 10 minutes before the sun went down completely. Twilight wasn't ideal in unknown terrain. Removing his phone again he checked for a signal, there was none, nor any Wi-Fi signals.

He looked at the map and the layout of the land. He realised Reb was not taking him via the visible roads as they did not correspond with the blue line in any shape or form whatsoever. He was being directed across the fields and along animal tracks.

Ignoring the directions, he headed off to the first village, following the nearby road, gauging that it should be no more than forty minutes away. Reb had purposely marked out a route to avoid habitation, presumably to prevent Sam from alerting the residents and the authorities to the nefarious activities within the rocky range behind him.

As Sam was approaching the outskirts of the village, he heard the roar of a fast-moving vehicle a mile or so behind him. Looking back, he could see cones of lights heading in his direction. Judging by the height and the sound, it was a pickup or a four by four which had spotlights mounted on the top bar. The outermost lights swivelled ninety degrees, the arc of light shining into the nearby fields. Sam realised that there must be people on the back of the truck actively searching the fields. Judging the distance from the village and the speed of the vehicle that was approaching, Sam knew he would never make it in time. If he stayed on the road, then he might as well just stick a white fluffy tail on his arse, hop along the road and wait for the shotgun pellets to impact, and once he was in those lights there was no escaping.

'Shit'! Sam mouthed, not for the first time that day. He couldn't see any gateways nearby; he ran. The vehicle was gaining ground fast. The curvature of country road was giving Sam an advantage in that they had to slow down for them and there was no direct line of sight. However, it also meant he had further to run. Exiting around a bend he still couldn't see a gate or side road in the darkness.

Sam ran directly at the lowest part of the hedge, controlling his stride pattern. Throwing the backpack in front of him, in a technique that will never be accepted by the Olympic Committee, he dove over the hedge. It wasn't a substantial hedge and thankfully it didn't have a ditch in front of it or barbwire behind, as Sam only managed to clear it by a hair's breadth. He landed by tucking in his head, rolling his right shoulder underneath him, diagonally across his back and coming out into a commando roll. Running from a crouched position, he grabbed his bag and headed off across the field whilst wiping his stark white face and neck with the mud that now covered him from shoulder to hip. He ran on into the darkness, pumping his legs as hard as they could go. With the surety that he had just wiped fresh manure over his face, Sam muttered, 'Oh, I'm gonna make these bastards pay', as he spat a piece of crap from his lips.

Sam managed to make it across the pasture and through another gateway just before the spotlights illuminated the hedge he'd jumped over and started searching the field. He lay down behind the gate post, which was a large recycled railway sleeper. Keeping his partially darkened face low to the ground, he watched the pickup, which was now driving slowly, move along the road. The beam was not powerful enough to reach Sam's cover efficiently and he watched as it crisscrossed the grass in an erratic and inefficient manner. More lights lit up the sky, coming from the village. Sam heard engines roar into life and move off. He presumed that they were joining in the search for him. 'Two nil for Reb's plan', Sam conceded. Struggling to look at the napkin in the moonlight now that his night vision had gone, and not daring to use his torch, he formulated the quickest route to find the predefined path. Reb had apparently expected him to head to the nearest village and fail as there were extra landmarks on the map to give him his bearings. He hated being played and again swore under his breath.

~*~

Resting by a small stream after a long night's slog over unfamiliar terrain, Sam wearily estimated he was only ten minutes away from the derelict farmstead. He had eaten the sandwiches around midnight and drank the water sparingly. He didn't want to drink from the streams he passed as he immediately thought of the unknown contents of the barrels and worried about the toxicity levels in the area. He had managed to wash himself and clean his coat in a cattle trough, as the water was mains fed so he felt it reasonably safe to do so. Again, thinking of the barrels and how they would rust and eventually leak, Sam could not figure out why the locals farmed the area. Obviously the hired goons in the villages were not fully aware of their employer's actions.

At nearly five-thirty in the morning, it was still pre-dawn as Sam continued on. He was starting to feel the chill now that he had stopped, and he pulled the woolly hat down over the top of his ears. The early morning rays should start to lighten the sky over the eastern horizon soon.

Sam came upon the derelict farmstead, and after carefully watching it for ten minutes from the partial cover of a nearby hedge, he decided to perform a quick reconnaissance around the stone wall perimeter.

The derelict farmstead would have been a lovely, quaint, rural cottage with several outhouses and an extensive garden, which must now be grazed by the local sheep as all the foliage was trimmed low. The roof had collapsed on the main building, with signs of ancient fire damage on the remaining trusses and smoke stains marring the tops of the empty and lifeless structural openings.

As Sam started to climb over the low stone garden wall on the far side of his expected arrival, several things happened in such a quick succession that they were almost instantaneous. A shadow detached itself from the nearest outbuilding with a quick glint of silver in the morning sun. A barely audible 'pfft' whispered across the courtyard, and Sam felt as if he had been hit in the ribs by a sledgehammer. His body's auto reflex threw him backwards before he knew what had happened and he found himself lying on his back in the shadow of the wall. He could clearly see three glistening metal fletchlets protruding from his torso, three inches below his left pectoral. They seemed to shine even in the shade. The steady sound of boots walking over the yard, crunching on the small stones, brought Sam back to his senses.

'I assume you saw that over the feed?' an adenoidal voice said, getting louder as it approached. 'Three to the heart, I'm checking now, keep calm, do you want a souvenir?' A sallow-looking figure suddenly appeared, peering over the wall. The butt of a rifle set into the shoulder, the barrel moving upwards, only inches away from clearing the coping stone.

Sam acted on pure instinct; he knew his gun was out of action as that was the only thing that could have prevented the barbaric-looking projectiles from ripping through his body. He snatched the throwing knife from his left cuff and with a practiced right arm, threw it into the attacker's throat just as his weapon's barrel came into view. The assailant's eyes went wide in shock, a gurgle came from his lips and the rifle went 'pfft' again as three more fletchlets penetrated the ground near Sam's head. The force completely buried them in the soft soil.

Sam had grabbed the second knife, but in the fraction of a second it took to transfer it to his throwing hand, the aggressor's face vaporised in a spray of blood, bone, skin and brain matter which all erupted outward, covering the area in a grisly mist as the larger particles fell slightly to the right of where Sam lay. A wide, bloody, gaping hole, showing the interior of the aggressor's head, slowly slid from view as the body crumpled down to the ground. Sam held on to the second knife as he heard another set of feet sprinting across the yard.

A voice he recognised from the cell shouted out. 'Sam! Just hold on, help is coming. Bob, patch me through to Control. Control, Reb, incursion, I need a medic and backup at the old cottage, stat.'

A craggy-faced, bald head cautiously appeared over the wall, and Sam's arm tensed ready to throw.

'Wow, easy soldier! Control, Sam is down, repeat, Sam is down, but he's alive.'

'What the hell's going on and tell me why I should not kill you right now?' Sam said vehemently, knife poised to throw. He moved his left hand to remove the fletchlets.

'Stop! Don't move. Move your hand away from the darts. Whoever this was, he clearly didn't intend you to live. Those two-inch darts protruding from you are razor sharp from tip to fin. They're generally coated in something very fatal and at room temperature, the metal will start to dissolve. Not only does that remove the evidence, but it releases toxins that are so deadly as to be universally outlawed. It's not the choice weapon of a real assassin, but it's a firm favourite for contract killers.'

Sam paused, not quite knowing what to make of it.

'Sam, listen to me, this is not what we planned for. I need you to do as I say, you're still at risk.' He slowly started to climb over the chest high wall, a large bore nondescript pistol in one hand.

That sort of explains the hole in the guy's head, but where's the silencer, Sam thought as he started to rise.

'Hold it, Sam, stay still and remain in the shadows. I suggest you carefully remove your coat,' the stranger said, standing next to Sam. He holstered the gun beneath his jacket. 'Oh, my name's Reb by the way, pleased to meet you, again.' He turned around, scanning the area. 'Control, Sam is alive. Where are those troops? This is meant to be a secure area, and I want answers by the time we get back to the village.'

Sam pushed the blade of his knife into the soil as he squirmed out of the jacket, making sure the prongs were as far away from his skin as possible. 'He said heart, three to the heart. That doesn't sound like a competent killer to me.' Lifting his shirt, he saw the ugly pistol-shaped bruise forming and gingerly tested his ribs with the tips of his fingers.

'You have no idea how lucky you are, pure luck you had your pistol there and even luckier that he didn't know about human physiology,' Reb replied, as he offered his hand to help Sam up. Sam gripped it and was almost lifted upright in a natural motion that didn't even alter Reb's balance.

'Leave your jacket and come over here,' Reb said, as he placed a hand on the wall and nonchalantly leapt across, one foot briefly touching the apex for balance as he did so.

As Sam climbed over, he paused at the top to examine the corpse below him. The man was dressed in dark grey clothing and one hand still remained firmly clasped to an odd-looking rifle. A small box on the top, similar to the electronic sights that Sam was used to, was suddenly crushed, the electronics viciously pushed into the ground by Reb's boot.

'Camera.' Reb informed him. 'He was being monitored by his employer. Someone really wants you dead, Sam, and I don't understand why. You're a nobody, no one had even heard of you until the other week. You have no strategic value, but he was here waiting for you. To be more precise, he wasn't here an hour ago when I arrived, checked and cleared the area.'

'You said human physiology, how could he get that wrong? Who are you?' Sam spun around to face Reb. He was getting angry now. He'd been lied to, electrocuted, held prisoner and now shot.

'Wake up Sam, for Christ's sake. You're not in Kansas anymore. You are standing on a piece of land approximately eighty miles in diameter that doesn't exist on any of your maps. You have just been shot at by a man that miraculously got past a garrison full of alert troops. He appeared from nowhere, and he had gills on the back of his neck.' He indicated that Sam should look.

Sam looked at the body on the floor. Blood had smeared down the stone wall where it had slid to the floor. It was now lying face down, the collar of the grey jacket partially obscuring the cadaver's neck. Sam wiped the knife blade on his jeans to clean off the soil and used the tip of the blade to move the collar aside. At the back of the dead man's neck were five slits on each side, reminiscent of shark gills. He opened one carefully with the blade, mucus strung itself between the slit lips, the insides were a greyish pink.

'I don't fu–' Straightening up, Sam was cut short by a faint beep, followed by a sizzle and an immediate rise in temperature. Reb grabbed Sam's collar and waistband and threw him a dozen feet across the courtyard with incredible strength. Two gun shots rang out in quick succession as Sam landed in a roll, springing to his feet with the knife still in his hand. He looked back at and saw Reb hastily kicking something away from the body. The body which was glowing from the centre mass and burning up inch by inch as a flameless orange ribbon flowed outward. Within the space of ten seconds, there was nothing left but black ash, a tarnished rifle and the smell of burnt flesh.

Reb put his finger to his ear. 'Are you seeing this, Bob? Get a tech down here. Tell him I managed to save the left hand for analysis.'

Sam looked at the item Reb had kicked across the courtyard. It was a hand and forearm. The forearm had been shot off at the elbow, and there was a broken trail of blood leading back to Reb. There was a strange branding on the underarm above the wrist. Five short lines, almost making a triangle, two lines per side.

'Ok, that got my attention, I'm listening,' Sam said.

'Sorry if I was a bit rough, Sam. Poor bugger, he probably didn't know this was a one-way trip. Whomever this guy's employer was, he had no intention of the man surviving to tell the tale. There couldn't have been an exit route from here, only the ECE, Energy Cascade Erasure. That burning glow is a form of raw energy that devours all organic tissue, it doesn't stop until it runs out of fuel. If you had been touching him...' Reb left the words hanging as he walked towards the hand, and rubbed the toe of his boot on some weeds to remove a splattering of blood.

Removing a small device from his pocket, he knelt down and scanned the hand and arm. A green line of light, similar to a bar code scanner, automatically roamed around the appendage, concentrating on the strange triangle. After a few seconds, Reb put the device away. 'Bob will have his ID and details sent to the station by the time we get there; we should move on. We can leave this mess for the clean-up team.'

'Reb, you still haven't told me what is going on.' Sam started to shiver. The pale morning sun was up but without his coat, it was bloody freezing.

'Ok, ok, in short, we are part of the Specialised

Universe Militarised Police Force. Our task is to protect and hide areas such as this,' he said, waving his arms around, 'from falling into the wrong hands. I will explain about that later. We are also the backup of any planetary system police. If they cannot deal with a problem, then we get called in. If our guys need backup, I, or my counterparts, get called in. Are you with me so far?' Reb enquired, moving on before Sam could answer. 'Everything that has happened to you in the last twenty-four hours, except this,' indicating the ash and the hand, 'was staged to see how you performed. You showed promise, you are inquisitive, intelligent and capable. We need a human on the team, and we were auditioning you. This is, was, a job interview.'

'Everything? The escape from jail, being hunted by the locals?' Sam asked.

'Escape! Don't make me laugh, we are tougher, faster and stronger than you are. They were playing with you at the guard house, to see how you performed and measure your personal boundaries. Sergeant Alcaeus' knee has been fixed by the way, and he asked me to tell you he is looking forward to your future training. He's our martial arts master and not the dumb, slow yokel that he masterfully portrayed. You will be training under him in future.'

'Training? For what? What are you talking about?'

'You'll be happy to know he doesn't hold a grudge by the way. Quite the opposite, he thinks you have potential. Hell, previously you managed to kick him in the jewels when you should have still been in a drugged stupor. Breaking his knee showed a controlled non-lethal use of force to incapacitate an aggressor. Let's say you passed that test. Staff Sergeant Timon was a little upset, as he was under duress to participate in the charade, to begin with. He doesn't think humans are adroit enough to be of any use, and I don't suppose the lads leaving him in the cell for an hour or so to cool down, helped his mood.' He chuckled to himself.

'What about the drums and the radiation suits?'

'Oh, they're real. But not what you think. We have to live on your planet, because of areas such as this. You humans are deplorable, you will pollute, destroy and desecrate anything if there is profit to be made. We are intercepting toxic waste that was bound for illegal disposal and disposing of it safely. That is what I was going to show in the mountain. That's what this was ultimately leading to.'

'So, you are dumping stuff in the mines, then?'

'No, we have a unique method of dealing with it. It's at the centre of this area, the reason for its creation and why we guarding this place. You will have to trust me and wait until you see it before you judge us.'

'So, you police us?'

'No. We would like nothing more than to remove or cull your criminal fraternity. However, as it was decreed a long time ago that your planet is segregated from the rest of the universe, we are here solely to protect and prevent access to areas such as this, from you and outsiders. We do hamper them a little, though. We frequently move money from crime lords to prevent them from becoming too powerful. We often divert the money to good causes, and we tip off your authorities.'

Three Toyota Land Cruisers arrived; men armed with machine pistols disembarked and took up strategic positions around the cottage. Three proceeded to check the house for further intruders, a fourth with a steel case walked over to Reb and following the nod of his head, proceeded to examine the hand. 'You haven't left me much to work with, Erebos,' he said, looking at Reb indifferently. 'Where's the rest?'

'ECE.'

The man picked up the bloodied hand and ragged stump, looking enquiringly at Reb.

'Had to shoot it off!'

'Ok, well I can't tell you much more than you know already until I get it back to the lab. A career criminal, mostly minor judging by penal triptych. He only had one-sixth left. Ergo he will be in the system. He was a eunuch, and if he wasn't in prison, which obviously he wasn't, it should have been impossible for him to leave his home planet.' He moved the arm around and studied the fingers, moving them in the morning sun to catch the rays and finally sniffing at them. He seemed oblivious that blood was dripping onto his jacket and boots. Looking across the ground to the ashes, 'The rifle probably won't tell us much, but I'll get the usual test run on it.'

'There are three darts in Sam's coat over the wall, they might have dissolved by now,' Reb said.

'There's three in the ground by my jacket, you can just about see where they went in,' Sam interjected.

The tech nodded to one of his men, who walked to the wall to look over.

'Do we know how he got here yet?'

'No, I checked the area an hour before Sam arrived. He was not here then, and I would have heard him if he walked across the courtyard,' he replied, looking down at the loose stones and gravel that littered the cobbled courtyard. 'But that's beside the point – he couldn't be here! It's impossible.'

'Erm, give me a minute, I need some equipment from my car.' He ran off to the middle car, opened the back door and rummaged around in a larger silver case. He returned within a few minutes with an odd-looking gadget, strewn with antennas and with a small screen showing various waveforms. Removing his own watch, he said, 'Give me your watch, Reb.'

Reb looked at him and held up a bare wrist. 'I lose it every time I travel,' he said as if the explanation made sense. The tech looked at Sam's wrist and snorted derisively. Walking to the wall, he spoke to the tech who was dealing with Sam's jacket.

Upon his return, he held two similar military issue analogue watches on leather straps.

'What are you up to, Nik?' Reb enquired.

'Bear with me.' He started the stopwatches simultaneously. Handing one to Reb, he walked off to the cottage, studying the glowing screen on his equipment.

Watching Nik walk away, Sam turned to Reb. 'Erebos?'

'From what you would call Ancient Greek, or I should say Ancient Latinised Greek. Your ancient Greek and Latin are our original native languages. We are given our life names after we qualify for our careers. Life names can change, as do the paths of life; birth names are private and a constant. Erebos means primordial darkness, as that is where I am sent, to blend, conquer and destroy.'

'That was a bit more than I expected. Look I'm confused, I'm trying to take this in, but...' He paused, not knowing where to start. 'What's this penal triptych?' Sam asked.

Reb turned the arm over to show the penal branding on the forearm. 'The triptych is made up of three sides, in six parts, a triangle. A criminal is awarded sixths depending on the severity of a crime along with some form of penal punishment. If you fill one side, you lose the ability to procreate – you are sterilised. Let's face it, society does not want to support a criminal's future family and nor do they make good parents. If you fill up two sides, you lose your genitalia and the ability to copulate. It's amazing how that threat can incentivise and keep you on the straight and narrow. The third side means you are removed from society forever. Similar to America's "three strikes and you're out" policy.'

Nik could be seen wandering in the outhouses, waving his gadget out in front of him. Eventually, he headed back to Sam and Reb.

'The results are not what you want to hear, Reb.' He held his stopwatch next to the one in Reb's hand; they no longer matched.

'We have a big problem,' he said, holding the severed arm and pushing the fingers towards Reb for him to see. 'You can just about see the early stages of temporal displacement degeneration at the ends of the fingers. It starts in the extremities. This is its very onset, an hour, two tops.' Reb and Sam leant in closer to examine the fingers; they were finger-like to Sam. Nails had been bitten down, and the bloke should have used a moisturiser, besides this, they were just dead man's fingers.

'So what are you saying, Nik?' Reb enquired.

'You didn't see him because he wasn't there when you arrived. He stepped through and not just through, he had no receiver at this end, and he stepped backwards in time. He was a dying man the second his foot touched the outhouse floor. HE is not going to like this!' He looked at Reb; there was the certainness of impending doom in his face. 'It also means we have a leak. At some point now or in the future someone talks out about this place, about Sam.' He looked bewildered at Sam then continued. 'It will have to be an insider, that rifle couldn't have come through. He,' morbidly pointing the dead hand at Sam, 'must do something. Something big that a major player wants to be undone. We only covered this briefly and only in theory at the academy, Reb. This is beyond my level. You're gonna have to get Bob to get more information released from the council and get us clearance. They sealed off all the files into this eons ago and outlawed any further research. The only other thing I can remember is that it takes so much energy they said it wasn't doable.'

'Are you hearing this, Bob?' Reb had his finger in his ear again. 'Ok, we will head back with Nik, see what you can do.'

CHAPTER 6

Nik carefully inserted the hand and forearm into a long plastic evidence bag and dropped it in his case. 'I'll have a full set of tests done. We know there's degradation, and someone went to a lot of trouble to try and dispose of the evidence,' he said as he opened the car door.

Sam and Reb sat in the back. Reb rightly concluded that Sam would have more questions to ask before they got to the village.

Sam's head was spinning with questions and the implausibility of what he had seen. 'How can this place exist and no one knows about it? I searched the aerial photos on Google Maps, and there was only a quarry cliff behind the warehouse.'

Reb smiled, 'Spatial distortions of this magnitude are hard to fathom at first, Sam. I will explain it as best as I can, but please remember I am not a scientist.' He looked across to Sam who just nodded in acquiescence for him to proceed. 'Certain events in the Earth's history caused ginormous distortions to the fabric of space. Think of Einstein's gravity wells and how space is like a rubber sheet. Your scientists have used this model for a long time. Let us pretend that the Earth is a balloon, and our finger is the gravitational disturbance; push it into the balloon. The balloon is still the same shape, only now the part where your finger is has stretched the outer fabric. You have more surface area and a small hole at the top. Now imagine that instead of a finger, it's a very, very small object. You still have the spatial distortion, only the hole at the top is minuscule. That's what this place is; there is a spatial distortion in the mountain. The sun is paler and cooler because the light enters from a small area and is distributed; it gets bent into the hole. Don't ask me why we don't get crushed, slide to the bottom or even why the earth doesn't shatter, because I don't know.'

'And you live in these planetal depressions?'

'We prevent access to the area, but we are here primarily to prevent access to the distortion at the centre. Your planet has 14 such areas.'

'You have villages and farms in all of them? Like this? And no one has noticed?'

'We have settlements in thirteen of these. The fourteenth, we have never been able to find the aperture. We know it's there as we can measure the disturbance, but so far it has eluded us.'

'So whereabouts is that one?'

'It's in the North Atlantic, and I mean in the North Atlantic, it's under the ocean somewhere.'

The journey to the village took less than ten minutes. Sam was a little reluctant to exit as the heat was blowing into the vehicle from the vents and making Sam more than a little tired. It had been a long twenty-four hours. The village was larger than he had expected, with straight streets of uniformed stone buildings radiating out from the centre hub like spokes on a wheel.

Reb had been talking to Bob in a hushed murmur. As he finished, Sam asked. 'Surely you have a better system than having to put your finger in your ear?'

'It's not necessary in truth. Bob listens and monitors my actions constantly. Pressing the micro button allows him to know that I am speaking directly to him and also prevents people around me from getting confused.'

'Speaking to yourself with your finger in your ear prevents confusion? Ok, sorry, so you have privacy then. You two must be close!'

'Bob, or that's what I call him, is my off-planet partner. He was assigned to me when I took up the uniform, and we have worked together ever since. I will be honest and admit that I have no idea what he looks like as we have never met. For security reasons I don't even know what race he is or where he is stationed. His guidance has saved my life on so many occasions that I no longer ask, I just accept it.'

They disembarked from the Land Cruiser and walked towards a drab four-storey round building, with a sturdy but functional look that was typical of most governing bodies. As they entered, Sam was reminded of all of the barracks and army buildings he had ever entered; he felt oddly at home. As a familiar but authoritative figure in uniform came forward to meet them, Nik excused himself as he wished to process the arm as soon as possible. The old man greeted Reb like a trusted friend and ushered them into a side office.

The office was functional, containing a large wooden round table that was surrounded by eight chairs. The furnishings showed signs of long-term use. It was all worn but extremely solid-looking furniture. On the table was a green folder with a large paperclip securing a photograph. The last time Sam had seen that face it was peering over a wall at him. Next to it was a thicker blue file with Sam's photo.

The man said, gesturing with his arm, 'Please sit down.' Nodding towards Sam, he said, 'Nice to see you again Sam, I am glad you made it to the party.' Returning his gaze to Reb, 'The details on the perpetrator have come through as you requested Reb, there is also a 'Classified' file waiting on the system. You will have to go to the Comms room to access it later.'

'Sam, this is Captain Sophus, I believe you two met in the hamlet garden. He's in overall command here. His duty is to protect this area and to maintain food production for other non-terrain locations.'

The captain stretched over and offered his hand to Sam.

'Hus, you already know this is Sam, and I take it that you have read his file.'

'My file?' He reached across to retrieve the blue file.

'Sorry, Sam, we had to do an in-depth background check on you when you reappeared the second time. It was only then you piqued Reb's interest. Luckily for you that he was here and noticed your tenacity and intelligence. Your military records hint that you might be what we are looking for. We need a native on the team.'

'You have my military records. All of my military records!' It wasn't as much of a question as a fact.

'We have everything, Sam,' Captain Sophus said. 'Your governments have made our research easier now everything is networked. Your best encryption is on par with a child hiding his favourite toy under the bed. We have your military files, police files, dental records, copy of your birth certificate, your social profiles, bank details and your purchase history. Interestingly your own government has recently done a background check on you – did you know Matt Johnson's company is a front for MI5? He has some very influential clients, you know.'

Sam looked hard at the old man, returning his gaze back to the file to find the corroborate evidence to this claim.

Reb reached for and opened the green file, pulling two printed sheets of A4 and a collection of photographs. 'Urser Moorc, A Gleesheatcian, multi-gas breather. Currently alive and well, serving time for drug running and assault. He was awarded fifteen native or eight ISPAW years for his recent activities and as usual, his assets were also confiscated.' Looking at Sam's enquiring gaze, 'To pay for the penal system fees and it earned him a whole triptych side. Which consequently also qualified him to lose his genitalia. Current photo as of two hours ago shows him alive and well.' He passed a black-and-white video still across to Sam. Urser could clearly be seen in ankle chains working some industrial machine. 'They have to work hard if they wish to obtain extra food, heat, clothing and even communal time to converse with others. The motto 'Penal is not a Picnic' holds true.'

Sam pushed the picture back. 'Nik mentioned a temporal thing before; are you saying this man, in the future, comes back to kill me?'

'The DNA scan and data embedded in the triptych that Nik sent through earlier matches the file.'

'Urser isn't the problem, Sam; he was a tool for a larger player, if not him then some other patsy. You don't comprehend the enormity of the situation. Time travel isn't normal, even for us.' Reb looked Sam in the eyes as he spoke. 'You heard what Nikomedes said, all temporal research of any kind is prohibited. Bob confirmed that it's an instant death penalty for anyone involved in research. Again, as Nik said, we personally know very little about the theory and what to look for.' He left the statement hanging.

'There must have been other instances in the past?' Sam asked, giving a questioning look to both Captain Sophus and Reb.

'If there were, they would have been classified. What we are allowed to know will be in the file waiting for Reb,' Captain Sophus said wearily. 'My concern is why you and why such a drastic action to remove you? If you do enlist with us, and if you wish to survive, as I suggest you do, they will get plenty of opportunities to take you out in the years ahead. Unless they have tried, failed and lost valuable resources. Then as a last resort at some indiscernible point in the future, they risk tipping their hand to the size and scale of their operation by attempting a temporal assassination.'

Reb stood up. 'Well, gentlemen, I think we need to see what's in the other file. For better or worse, you might as well join me as you are both involved.'

The communications room was a bit of a let-down in Sam's eyes. He had imagined huge arrays of data banks and complicated encryption equipment. It consisted of an array of iMacs, printers and a few headsets scattered along a large C-shaped work area. Sam was expecting a scene from Star Trek and said so.

'When we go native, we go native! We use your so-called technology as much as possible, that way when we are outside the perimeter we are familiar with the tools that are readily available.' The captain was a little put out as he described the situation to Sam. 'We don't like taking our tech outside. Take Reb's side arm, for example; he can have any number of energy blasters or projectile weapons off-world, but here he chooses a modified Heckler and Koch 45. To the naked eye, it's a vanilla HK piece, but we borrowed the blueprints, increased the accuracy, range, reduced the recoil with better compensators and upgraded the munitions.'

'I didn't hear it go off at the house?'

'The ammo uses a modified cordite propellant, a very low explosion to compressed gas expulsion ratio causing a subsonic round. There's no need for a noise suppressor.'

He walked into the middle of the room, 'But I get your point,' he said, smiling. 'I think you'll like this.' He commanded, 'overlay of non-indigenous life forms within the perimeter.'

A colourful transparent three-dimensional image flowed down from the ceiling around him, projecting a circular terrain complete with rivers, hills and several hundred moving red dots to symbolise the non-indigenous life forms.

'Overlay indigenous humanoid life forms.'

An orange dot appeared within a tiny ethereal building next to two red ones. The captain placed his hand near the building's corners and stretched the image to enlarge it. He then circled the room containing the three dots and asked, 'Identify.'

'Three bipedal life forms are present in the selected area,' a seemingly omnipresent but strangely familiar voice said. 'Two Minerans and one human. In order of rank: Agent Erebus, identification number is classified, Captain Sophus, identification number 5973epsilon 6254theta 1235Chi and Sam Shepard, guest identification Gamma 701, his security status is classed as mostly harmless.'

Sam looked at Captain Sophus. 'Why do I recognise that voice?'

'Native Film night this week was Pulp Fiction. We analyse your media to learn more about you and your cultural evolution. Your planet's culture is multifaceted and evolves so quickly; it's actually fascinating. Nik likes to change the audio theme of the AI, this week she's Uma's fictional character, Mia. We had a woman from Blade Runner for a whole year once. He loves your concept of what we should be like, he even maps out parallels.'

While this was going on, Reb had accessed a console and read the awaiting report. He looked up as Hus closed the holographic display down. 'Apparently there are automated monitoring outposts out there, and they can usually trace new research facilities via the particular gravitational disturbance they cause. It seems they ripple out from the epicentre, allowing triangulation. Nineteen instances are on record since the council's formation. They were all eradicated within three hours. Mostly the buildings they were housed in were purged, but there have been instances where the laboratory was buried so deep inside the planet that the whole city, or in one case, the entire world, was destroyed. It doesn't say who enforces this and Bob isn't saying either – I am afraid we are still in the dark.' He stood up and looked at Sam. 'Clearly someone has created a method, and they have had long enough with it to be able to send Urser through. We do not know when from or where. We wouldn't see the ripples as they haven't happened yet. There is some data on symptoms; we saw some degradation on Urser's fingers, and we have the schematics to create a detector which I can pass onto the techs. Besides that...' He raised and shrugged with his arms to indicate there was nothing else to do.

'Nik's forensics might come up with a few things. Age of the future Urser, for one, and any pathogens that might be in the blood to indicate which planets he recently visited,' the captain said. 'Reb, take Sam for some food, get him cleaned up and take him inside the mountain. Finish showing him what you set out to do.

CHAPTER 7

They didn't go to the main canteen; Reb opted to walk to the local tavern instead. As they vacated what Sam assumed was the headquarters building, he looked back at it. It took up all of the central hub. It had small windows which were recessed back by about a foot. The glass looked thick. The door they exited from was the only doorway visible on this side – it was not so much an office building, more of a fortification, Sam realised.

'A little out of place for such a laid back, back to nature area?' he enquired.

'Standard HQ design. It's the same in every enclave.' Looking back at the building, Reb replied. 'Four levels above ground, thirty levels below. Nothing you have could scratch it, never mind crack it open. It can house, feed and look after every enlisted man here for two years. It taps into the earth's mantle for geothermal energy and heat. The machine floor can manufacture anything as long as you feed it a schematic. No one stays there at the moment as most prefer the building they built themselves, only temporarily relocating for duty rosters or battalion manoeuvres. You can think of us as highly trained policing settlers; mostly we grow food and are at one with the area. Ultimately we are here to prevent it from falling into the wrong hands and the odd off-world assistance. That's why I was here the other week, I'd required the skills of Apate for a few days and had just returned with her when you popped up.'

~*~

They had walked a fair way down the street which was wide enough for four normal lanes, the houses were set back with small ornate gardens. A larger building ahead had a traditional weather-beaten sign outside declaring it to be the "Pig-inn Barrel", with a faded picture portraying a large upright beer barrel. In the barrel stood a lean pig in the quasi-police uniform holding a double-barrelled weapon pointed forward. The end of the double-barrel resembled a snout.

'Strange sense of humour for aliens?' Sam's inflection making it a question rather than a statement.

'Policing InterGalacticaly. It's a semi-offensive nickname. It's not very accurate as the force covers the whole of the unified universe. We take the small blessing that they don't call us Puu.'

'So you have pigs in space then?'

'Evolution is amazing, Sam, so many permutations and designs, but with so many planets, repetition on similar planets is quite normal. Your pig looks similar to various species called "pig". We gave you the name for the animal, well for most of your animals. Don't forget, visually we look similar.'

They entered the establishment through a heavy oak door, the warmth reminding Sam that he was still without a jacket and this place was consistently cold. The interior looked like any other local hostelry, only cleaner, larger and in good condition. Large oak tables with solid oak chairs and comfy-looking padded seats were scattered around the airy room. Sam could smell the aroma of freshly baked bread. His stomach grumbled to remind him that he hadn't eaten much in the last twenty-four hours.

Reb led them to a table by the window and ordered both of them a large brunch. 'Bob has arranged for you to have a room here for a few hours, you can freshen up and grab some sleep after breakfast.'

Sam ran his fingers through the stubble on his chin and nodded. 'The AI called you Minerans, why?'

'Our planet of origin is called Minera. When we settled here a long time ago, we named it after our home. Earth was our first assigned planet and Minera was the first colony. There will be Minerans here forever until your sun goes supernova. We choose, to a degree, where we are stationed, but all of our children must be born and raised back on Minera. They only leave the home world when they become of age and enlist.'

Sam realised that he hadn't seen any children. The hamlet shop, or should he say NAAFI, as that was what it had subconsciously reminded him of, hadn't stocked anything for them. 'Do you mean your whole race is sworn into service? And that you work for an all-powerful planet destroying government? If you think this is making me want to sign up, you are sadly mistaken.'

A stout man with a metal torc around his neck arrived and deposited a tray of food on the table. Reb nodded in appreciation and continued talking to Sam.

'Sam, you must understand firstly we are not like your planet. Our government's first...'

Sam interrupted Reb with a questioning look and by silently pointing at the barman indicating the collar around his neck.

'Ah Emliton, huh, don't panic he's not a slave or anything like that. He suffers from narcolepsy.' Seeing more confusion on Sam's face, he continued, 'A sleep disorder, he nods off at the drop of a hat during the day. The neck band vibrates when his chin sags to wake him up, he made it himself. Em is the only non-combatant in the enclave, he more than makes up for this by being a master brewer and distiller. He also makes all of our ethanol and biofuel for the vehicles.'

Picking up his plate and cutlery from the tray he continued, 'As I was saying, the government's first priority is to prevent corruption from within. Then it sorts out external corruption and only then can it try to govern the universe fairly and maintain order. Their sanctity is to remain pure, unadulterated and to be able to prove it, it has to have total transparency of its actions and goals. All government employees are financially audited every year: income, expenditure, capital assets, holidays, etc. From the Chief Executive down to the lowest file clerk. No one is allowed to take bribes, secondary jobs or accept gratuities. They are audited for life to prevent delayed payments. It is all very strict, and there are no second chances if you are proven to be corrupt or to have taken a bribe; you and your family are punished for life. The sentence is that all of your assets are ceased, and you are all relocated to a colonial outpost. There are few luxuries on such outposts, and none of the family members may hold a position of authority. The corrupt employee himself may also face more severe punishment. It has seldom happened to rogue government workers, but there are terraforming planets where the most heinous of criminals spend the rest of their solitary lives. They live in terraforming pods miles from anywhere with set tasks to complete every day to obtain food and basic luxuries such as music and reading material from the AI. It is a bleak existence, spending most of the day outside in an environment suit tending the terraforming plantations, never having enough oxygen to travel to the next pod. They will never see another living being again.'

'Terraforming plantations?' Sam enquired as he cut into a large, juicy, pork-filled sausage. He hadn't realised he was quite so hungry. 'These are good, by the way.'

'All of the food we eat is grown here or at the other enclaves. It's fresh, pure and unadulterated. It'll be the best sausage you taste on this planet,' Reb remarked, quickly changing the topic, he continued, 'We have the technology to terraform a planet mechanically. However, these systems require massive resources, and they pollute the planet as much as they terraform. The Overseer has given us a lot of technological advancements. One of them being the blueprints showing how to use natural vegetation from different planets to slowly change atmospheric types over the course of a thousand years or so. It can take several of these cycles to get to the atmosphere you require. It's a long, drawn-out process. No right-minded person would have dreamt up such a scheme. It is very effective, it's a fraction of the cost in money, and it doesn't use up any of the planets natural resources. It also acts as a humane penal system for lifers, they grow their own food, and there is no escape. At the end, you get a new planet for colonisation.'

The serving man returned with another tray with a selection of refreshments: a coffee cafetière, a pig teapot and fresh juice. 'I took the liberty of also bringing some fresh tea for Sam,' he said. 'Xenophon's reports stated that he noticed Sam typically favoured a strong breakfast tea.' He placed a marble on the table in front of Sam. 'Phon said to say he looks forward to meeting you in person. Apparently, you have amused him.' He walked off, taking the empty tray with him.

Reb smiled as Sam picked up the marble. 'I'd take that as a compliment, but he will get you back. Phon has turned into a bit of a joker, he's spent too much time outside amongst your kind.'

'Sorry, exactly who hasn't read my file? The barman? Really?'

Laughing, Reb picked up a slab of freshly baked bread that had been toasted until it had a uniform golden brown crust and then slathered in salted butter. 'You could be fighting alongside anyone of them in the future. They have a right to know what makes you tick. Each and every one of them has a file that is open to all that serve here. Apparently, Apate's medical footage caused quite a stir. Most of them have never seen a naked human before, she was quite thorough,' he finished, still smiling.

Thinking back to his B&B and how he must have slept through God knows what, Sam said, 'She's a medic, then.'

'No, she volunteered to plant the rather obvious camera and for expediency perform a medical examination for the doctor.' Reb was clearly enjoying himself as he tried to hide his laughter by stuffing the toast into his mouth. 'Look, we digress, and you have to comprehend where we are coming from to make an informed decision.'

Clearing his mouth with a swig of coffee he continued, 'As you can imagine, there are not many civil servants who misbehave. In ISPAW, greed and power are not the motives of a good politician. That type of individual seldom makes it through the selection process. Why should they, they won't earn any more money than they would as a serviceman.'

'Serviceman?'

'All of our wage systems are based around service pay. An individual who puts his life on the line and serves, is worth more than a banker, statesman or, as is the case on your planet, a so-called celebrity or footballer. There are wage bands above this of course, but no one will ever receive three times more than the ordinary soldier or police officer. Which brings us nicely to the requirements and criteria for an individual who wishes to register for any elected role in the government body. Whether it's his planetary government or part of the Inner Sphere Parliament of Aligned Worlds, ISPAW, the individual has to have served as a serviceman in one of the forces and the length of time varies depending on his or her species. It ranges from 10 to 25% of life span. For instance, for you humans, it would be approximately 18 years in service, and you would have to have obtained the minimum rank of, er, what's the term you use, Warranty Officer or above.'

'Do you mean Warrant Officer? It's the highest non-commissioned rank in the British Army.'

'Warrant Officer, yes that's the one. Sorry, it is hard to keep track as you have so many separate armies for one small world. Consolidating them would be more economical, you know!'

Laughing, Sam replied, 'I don't think that is going to happen, Reb. So what you are saying is that they all have to serve in the Army to come out as a gung-ho politician?'

'Not exactly, there are also the other forces. Medic, Pyro and the Protection, the police. The terms served with these are greater as they are considered to the larger extent as non-lethal vocations. Then having gained suitable life experience and served the greater good they have to enrol in an academic institute to gain the knowledge to actually go into politics. The system pays for this so as to make it available to all, not just the wealthy.'

'So are you saying that after they have proven themselves to be worthy by serving their country, well, planet, system or whatever, you then suck out their scruples and morals at some academy? You do know Britain's suffered from all the Ruperts that have come out of Oxford and Cambridge. Different parties, same education and ideology.'

'Very cynical, Sam, please do not judge us by your planet's malfeasance and nepotism. You are, as I said before, a cesspit of corruption, on such a scale that we have not seen the like of in several millennia. That's only because we are expanding outward and absorbing new systems and cultures. Internally we have not seen this level since the Overseer's purge.'

'Sorry, you mentioned this Overseer before, who's he? How did he get all the power?' Sam dabbed his mouth with the supplied napkin. He was comfortably full and feeling slightly tired. He stirred the tea in the pot, noting the aroma of the dark leaves as he did so. 'Tea?' indicating Reb's teacup.

'No, thank you,' picking up his coffee mug, 'I'll stick to the coffee. An astute question and one which I do not have a full and complete answer for. The truth is no one actually knows who he, she or they are. But they are powerful, more than you can comprehend. He, and we for some reason do call the Overseer a singular he, the 'Overseer' was the name he chose, and it seems to have male connotations. He brought order from chaos over 10 billion years ago. Most of the races were constantly at war with each other, competing for habitable planets and resources. The death rate was astronomical, and they began to develop weapons that could tear the fabric of space apart. Much like your own world, the ruling governments and corporations were all corrupt. Their only agenda was to gain more power and riches. Whole planetary systems were enslaved, extorted or eradicated. It was our darkest hour on record. Then "He" spoke. To everyone at the same time, through every communication device, in every language across the entire universe. "Cease or be destroyed". Of course, he was ignored – who could face any of these mighty armies, let alone all of them? Within two hours of his message every combatting armada, army or fighting individual was gone, vanished; no wreckage, no distress signals, no survivors, nothing. Accusations flew across the galaxies. Governments were scared of each other, bigger threats were made between the races, each blaming the next, fearing their neighbour had an unknown superweapon. So, new larger armadas were made. The more aggressive races started to use new, untested weapons, terrible devices that turned space in upon itself and ripped systems apart. There are areas of space that we cannot traverse, even now. The Overseer spoke again and upon being ignored, four densely populated home worlds of the primary antagonists and their armies vanished – and I mean disappeared. There should have been colossal wreckage, fragments of shattered planets spinning out in all directions, new asteroid fields and radiation. But no, it was like someone had just plucked them all from space like you pick an apple from a tree. This was power on an unheard of scale. Governments took notice and listened this time; they didn't want to be the next planet to inexplicably vanish.

The Overseer laid down the rules over the following centuries. Rules that we still adhere to today. He set up the ISPAW as the self-governing body; no race that joined the council could go to war with another. Any new race that we met on our expansion outwards was to be offered membership, left alone if non-spacefaring or isolated and annexed. Certain technology was prohibited like time travel, though this list is itself secret and only known to a small few as not to encourage people to investigate the topics. Each system is self-contained but has a seat on the Sphere's council. No system is allowed to use the council for self-gain. A few have tried over the eons and were dealt a swift and demonstrative punishment from The Overseer. We have never seen him, but every so often when someone steps out of line... They fear him, and that maintains order.'

'Oh come on. This is ridiculous, you're saying some godlike, ageless entity, over 10 billion years old, looks after everyone and basically acts as a primary school teacher for the universe.'

'A rather simplistic statement and the answer is yes and no. The Overseer claims no power and wants no homage. He quickly shuts down the zealots who tried to create religions in his name. I personally think it's an ancient race of beings that have been around far longer than us and are so far advanced that we will never catch up. Where and who they are, remains a mystery. They make themselves known only when we step out of line, and yes, I think they look upon us as children, nothing else makes sense. There are lots of historical docu-vids on the matter. I'll get you access to them once we get this sorted out.' Finishing his coffee, he eyed the last piece of toast. 'There were also seven new languages introduced to aid communication between races. Different types of communication depending on the physical ability of the race. There are several based on vibration frequencies, er, sound languages. There is also light, feel and smell based languages. You might be interested to hear that your own Queen's English is a bastardised version of Unilang One.'

'So English and the ancient Greek language are with your compliments then?' Pouring a second cup for himself, he needed to rehydrate his body.

'We have, over the centuries, tried to bring you into line with the ISPAW's standards, to make the transition easier for when you are intelligent enough to join. You might be amused, or maybe not, to find that most of your modern and ancient languages are alien to this world. Even though your planet is officially cordoned off because your populace is too retarded to join the Council. So, officially there should be no contact, no visitors, and no manipulation from off-world. However, the truth couldn't be further from that. Every major system has representatives here, working in the shadows of your governments and large corporations. Advising and dropping technological hints, just enough to lead you down certain pathways. If they are too overt, we can step in and clean up the mess.'

'So what have they given us, and why not just teach us all the same language?'

'Normally it's small technological advances, concepts and suchlike. And, because if one day, in the far, FAR future, you're deemed worthy enough to join the Council, they will already have a foothold here for trade negotiations. Let's put it in perspective, the information they give probably looks more advanced from your point of view. Let's imagine you saw an early Palaeolithic man picking up the first rock to club an animal. He's just about to discover how to reshape the rock, and you jumped in and showed him flint knapping just before he got there naturally. In his eyes, you have reshaped the next 3.4 million years commonly known as the Stone Age. You would be godlike in his eyes, but all you're really thinking is bloody primitives, can't even shape a stone. Well, that's what certain off-world factions are doing here. Primitive and simple technology, a hint of a chip design here, a chemical formula there. We only recognise the interference when the products are released. Occasionally we will pre-empt it if our deep network scans pull up suspect information.' Reb buttered the last piece of toast and picked up one of the tall glasses full of fruit juice. 'We, they, whichever, have maybe inadvertently altered and shaped your history from day one. Three-quarters of your modern languages can be traced to off-world cultures, either directly or indirectly. Hell, you didn't think French was a proper language did you?' He laughed. 'That's the nursery language for the Phlenenards.'

'Phelan... who?' Sam struggled to say the name.

'Phlenenards, their lava don't develop what they call higher brain functions for three decades. It's their infant talk, similar to your cutchycoo, binkie, booboo. A Phlenenard in his prime can out-compute any AI or array that I know of. Their young would have the mental capacity of your best scientists. The Phlenenards are literally organic computers on legs and bloody annoying to boot.' He looked across at Sam while stuffing a toasted corner into his mouth. 'Go and get some sleep, Sam. Someone will bring up some fresh clothes in a few hours, and we can continue our talk then.' He pointed to the stairway across the room. 'Go up the stairs, first door on the right. If you need anything just pick up the phone by the bed.' Reb got up and thanked the bartender as he left.

~*~

Stifling a yawn, Sam rose as the barman arrived to clear the plates. 'I'm hoping he hasn't stuffed me with the bill?'

'Not to worry Sam, this one's the Captain's tab,' he said with a wink. 'Nice to have you on board. I quite like the locals in these parts, you humans are so inquisitive. Still, what with your short lives and what not. What is it they say? The flame that burns twice as bright burns half as long, shame really.' With those morose words, he ambled off, carefully balancing the dirty plates on the tray.

Sam would later discover that the Overseer also gave ten complex equations, explaining that each equation, once fully understood, would enhance understanding and the quality of life for all. The first and easiest one to decipher, albeit only 82 per cent deciphered to date, was designed to humble the member planets of ISPAW. It described the reality that they lived in. It shattered any illusions of grandeur, describing the formation of the Universe not as a solitary event but one of the millions occurring in the immense void of space. They previously thought that a random act caused the formation of the universe; however, it was, in fact, the coalescence of matter produced by the collision of extreme energy particles passing through the void that we call space. Thus the universe was created, but not just the universe, the Infiniverse. These rare occurrences happened millions of times over in the timeless age of the endless void. It became known that the order of things was planet, solar system, galaxy, universe and Infiniverse, the gaps or voids between each becoming exponentially larger than the ones before. Not only did it describe a working model for the Infiniverse, it mathematically proved that the energy particles came from elsewhere, proving an existence or realm beyond current comprehension. It was thought that the remaining 18 per cent would describe what was beyond the Infiniverse. It must be noted that no member of the ISPAW had ever seen the edge of their ever expanding universe, so vast was its nature.

The partial decoding of the second equation led to an understanding that aided with the beginning of the third. They seemed to cover theoretical energy sources and a greater understanding of the building blocks of life. Neither the second or third equations had been deciphered past 15 per cent, even with three planets of Phlenenards working constantly on them. The other seven equations were so far beyond current understanding that only a few of the higher thinking systems could even consider the subject matter, let alone decode them.

The Overseer proclaimed that once the ten equations were understood, then the ISPAW would no longer need his guidance as they would have attained a sustainable enlightened level of consciousness.

Sam found the room easily enough. It, like the bar downstairs, had a rustic wood theme. The super-king-sized bed had stout wooden corner posts, and it was covered with a feather filled duvet. 'I could get used to comfort like this,' Sam said to no one in particular. He was too tired to worry about cameras and spy holes; if they wanted to view him showering, good for them.

Within fifteen minutes he was in bed, still slightly damp from his shower and smelling of beeswax from the rough block of soap. Most ex-military retained the ability to drop off at a moment's notice, and Sam was no exception. Even the light coming in through the open curtains failed to disturb his deep slumber.

CHAPTER 8

Sam awoke several hours later to the chirping of an alarm. He looked at the bedside cabinet to find that someone had placed a small digital alarm clock there with a folded note. Stretching, he let his finger crawl over the top of the clock until he found a depressible surface and pressed; he hoped it was the off button. Grasping the note, he brought it closer to read. 'Meet you downstairs in ten minutes. Reb.'

Sitting up he saw that his dirty clothes had been removed from the chair where he had left them and replaced, cleaned, on the cabinet. 'Jeeze, someone likes laundry duty,' he muttered.

He was happy to see his Scottevest jacket hanging on the back of the chair. From where he was sat, he could barely see the repair work covering the puncture marks.

He dressed quickly and found the suitcase with the rest of his belongings from the bed and breakfast at the foot of the bed. He was dismayed to find that his jacket had been stripped of all utilities, including his wallet, phone and gun. Sliding his arms into the jacket and shucking it over his shoulders he left the room, but not before making the bed. Old habits!

~*~

Reb, Nik and the captain sat at the previous table with mugs of steaming coffee in front of them. A spare mug sat in front of an empty chair. The captain offered it with a gesture of his arm. 'There will be a few sandwiches in a minute if you're peckish. I thought you should know the results from the test and we can answer any other questions you might have. We forget what it must be like from your perspective. This is all new and somewhat unbelievable. Reb will take you onto the mountain later and you can see the disposal of those barrels that you worried so much about. Once you are satisfied with that, we can get on with the more important matters, such as what you want to do. It is, after all, your choice if you wish to enlist. Also, we have a security issue. How did Urser know when and where to find you and how did he get in? Solving this conundrum is paramount. This enclave has never had an incursion before. Its location is a highly guarded secret, as are all enclaves; you can understand the significance of what I am saying.'

'It doesn't necessarily mean you have a traitor in your midst, anything could happen in the future to give away your position.' Sam picked up the mug of hot black coffee as he replied.

'I hope you are right, Sam, as only Minerans have ever manned this outpost and we don't like to think it's one of us.' Nodding to Nik, 'What does your report say, Nik?'

'Sadly not as much as you would like, I am afraid. We have determined that the arm is thirty-five and a half years older than Urser is today. That does not help us as the vascular tissue shows evidence of cryogenic fluid residue, meaning he has been on ice for an undeterminable amount of time. It could have been for a day, a year, or a decade, there is no way of knowing.'

'I thought cryofreeze had limitations, cellular degeneracy sets in after a few decades. Can't we use that to measure the period of time?' asked Reb.

'Well, yes and no, for two reasons. One, only commercially available units suffer from CD. The Council has had CD free systems for centuries. Two, the temporal degradation has made this impossible to gauge. The structure of the arm has broken down too much. It is, as we speak, no more than a length of jellified organic material. By tomorrow it will be a slurry. Shooting him was the kindest thing you could have done to him, Reb.'

'Actually, by the time I reacted he was already dead.' He slid a silver disc into the middle of the table. 'On.'

The round wooden table top was turned into a screen. Sam could still make out the wood grain through the ghostly blue image. It was a recording of the events at the decrepit cottage taken from above. Seeing Sam facially query, he answered, 'Orbital reconnaissance drones.'

Sam lifted his mug a fraction off the table again to see if the picture was beneath, it was. Reb touched the table and the video played. They could all see Sam arrive at the back courtyard, having circled round. A shadow moved from the outhouse as Sam approached the wall. The barrel of the weapon was clearly visible as the recoil caused it to glint in the low morning sun. Sam fell to the ground, stunned for a fraction of a second, his head looking along his prone body at the three protrusions sticking out of his midsection. Reb could be seen running from the far side of the building, gun in hand, a fraction of a second too late to prevent the assassin from bringing his weapon to bear. Sam's arms moved quickly, a flash of silver lanced across the screen to become lodged in the assailant's head. Reb touched the table top, and the picture froze. Sam was on the floor, the other knife in his hand ready to throw, the metallic handle protruding from Urser's head and Reb one step from clearing the corner of the building. Reb gestured with his hands on the table, and the picture zoomed down and angled to Sam and Urser. The thirty-degree angle alteration clearly showed Sam's throwing knife sticking out of Urser's throat. 'I have to give the credit to Sam, I didn't realise it at the time, but I would have been too late to save him. I have played the surveillance back for thirty days prior to this, and it is as Nik said. Urser seems to have just appeared into the outhouse building after I arrived and cleared the area.'

'Again that's not possible.' The captain looked from under his bushy eyebrows towards Nik. 'Nik, you need to sort this out, there should have been alarms going off all over the place. Reb, get Bob on it and see what the Council have to say. We are still working in the dark here, and I don't like it. The authorities will keep an eye on the present-day Urser and watch him carefully when he is released in a few years or so. Besides that, were there any leads in the blood?'

'No, someone has worked hard to obscure Urser's whereabouts. The blood had been through some form of dialysis. There were no foreign bacteria, pathogens or viral infections present. The only thing we could find before the tissue degraded was that he suffered from high cholesterol.' He looked across the table a little crestfallen. 'Sorry.'

'Not your fault, Nik, you can't find what's not there. We carry on as normal and hope they slip up at some point.' Getting up from his chair the captain took a sandwich from the platter that was being deposited on the table. 'Carry on, gentlemen.'

Stretching across, Reb used his fingers to inspect the repair work on Sam's jacket. 'Not bad for a rush job,' he proclaimed. 'Eat up, Sam, we have a busy afternoon planned,' he said while slathering a large beef sandwich with speckled and lumpy mustard. Putting the knife down on his plate, he continued, 'Oh, that reminds me.' He pulled a small box from under the table and handed it to Sam. 'You might want these'.

Sam tilted the box so he could see inside. There were two throwing knives, similar but not the same as his originals and a new Glock with three magazines. 'You're giving me my gun back?' he enquired.

'Not exactly. Yours was not repairable, Nik had this one fabricated as a replacement. The workshop will have improved on the original design, I think you'll approve,' he said with a smile. 'Be careful what you shoot at. These,' holding up one of the magazines, 'have more poke than you are used to. A friction reactive compound, blended into the metal slug, produces a small silent explosion. It propels the fragments into a controlled wide cone shape increasing trauma and tissue damage. We try to keep the compound levels low, as to make them undetectable to your forensics.' Smiling at Sam, 'You've seen the results, first-hand.'

Sam loaded and cocked the Glock, and inwardly sighed as the familiar and welcome weight settled in his jacket. Pulling the knives out of the box he looked at Reb.

'A superior alloy that doesn't corrode and it will keep its edge for longer.' He took hold of one of the knives. 'These are perfectly balanced for handle throwing and besides the finger loop for your cuff pockets, they are an exact copy of our standard tactical throwers.'

'Em, can you put the board on?' he shouted to the barman. After a few seconds, the wall in the far corner of the pub illuminated. Again, Sam could make out the wood grain behind the overlaid graphics. The board, as Reb called it, was eight feet wide and to the ceiling. It currently showed a large countdown timer starting from five. After it had hit one, the scene changed to portray a typical office environment. The scene moved in first person perspective and entered a doorway. Reb's arm swung in a lightning fast blur as a gun-toting balaclava masked figure appeared behind a hostage. The frame froze when the knife struck the wall, leaving the handle protruding from between the assailant's eyes. 'Help yourself if you want to try them out.' Sam looked across the bar room; the throw had been deadly accurate, over a distance of forty feet from a sitting down position. There was a faint white line on the floor by the bar which Sam walked up to. Taking position and slowing his breathing, he threw the knife over the twenty-five-foot span. The blade struck and barely penetrated into the hardwood behind the image, but he only managed to nick the top of the balaclava.

'Don't feel too bad, Sam, most of our recreational games are designed to hone our combat skills, and as I said, we are much stronger and faster than you.'

Sam retrieved his knives and returned to the table. The picture of a faceless Urser was still being displayed. Upon seeing the direction of Sam's gaze, Reb removed the metal disk from the table and replaced it into his pocket. The image faded as soon as the disk moved from the table. 'We'd better head off, I just need to pick up a few supplies for the Doc.'

They both walked across to the bar where Emliton

was sat on a stool, elbow on the polished wooden counter and his chin resting in the palm of his hand.

'Em, can we have the bottles for Doc?' As they drew alongside the barman, Reb nudged him awake. 'Wake up, Em.'

With a sudden snort, Emliton looked up, surprise showing in his eyes. 'Sorry Reb, must have nodded off, what did you say?'

CHAPTER 9

They walked back to the village centre, Reb carrying a small plastic-looking briefcase which Emliton had waiting ready behind the bar. 'I don't drink often, but you do need to try his ales. Hus went out of his way to entice Emliton here, despite his disorder. I don't believe his bluster about increased efficiency in fuel production for one second,' he laughed. 'Doc has a crate of pure distillate every week. You haven't met him yet. We thought for years that he had this huge alien-enabled drinking ability.' Holding up the case he said, 'This would kill you or me. It's 198 per cent proof or 99 per cent pure ethyl alcohol. Turns out he cleans himself with it. The station safety officer went ballistic when he found out, but he was overruled, bar a few precautions.'

Reb took them to the Toyota that they had used earlier. Sam rode shotgun with the case of volatile liquid on his lap. 'Is this stuff safe?' Sam enquired nervously.

'As long as you don't drink, inhale or drop it, you'll be ok,' Reb replied.

Reb gunned the engine into life with a mighty and

overdramatic roar. As he was about to drive off, the HQ door opened. Two guards in dress uniform stepped out, taking a position on either side as more stepped through. 'Sphericals, I was hoping we'd miss this,' he said, as a beautiful and nude woman stepped through, flanked by a guard on either side. Two males were similarly escorted. All three were clearly healthy and of a muscular build, no fat or cellulite could be seen. Not that Sam looked at the men, his eyes were drawn to the brunette as she walked past. She turned her head and looked directly into his eye.

'Isn't that...' He left the question hanging as Reb replied.

'Yeah. Living up to her name again, don't let her appearance deceive you. Apate has a wild, rebellious streak that hasn't been broken yet, but she is fiercely loyal and a good one to have covering your back. That's why she's here at the moment,' gesturing with his arms to mean Minera. 'As I said, we haven't long been back from an off-world mission and you re-appeared. If you join us, she will be a member of your team. Most of the people you have interacted with so far are here to evaluate you. They have dissected your life and put obstacles in your way to see how you react. They have been taking the measure of you to decide if they want to work with you.'

Sam watched as they were paraded under guard to a series of posts near a flat blank wall. Each prisoner took up a position in front of a post and stared calmly forward.

'I heard she struck a superior, putting him into the infirmary this morning with a broken nose and fractured cheek bone. The other two, I've no idea.'

Sam grabbed for the door handle, the other hand crashing through the breakout zip on his jacket pocket, fingers clasping around the pistol grip.

'Hold on, Sam! She doesn't need you to rescue her,

she'll be ok. Just watch.'

Twelve guards raised their rifles in unison, a firing line facing three unarmed and oddly compliant prey. It took a firm hold from Reb to convince Sam to sit still.

'I can't sit here and watch you murder them in cold blood. If you wanted me on your side, then this just screwed up your plans.' He spat the words out in the realisation that he could not break free from the immensely strong arm holding him to the seat. Jesus, this guy is strong, rang through Sam's mind, and he tried to formulate a plan.

'We are a quasi-military police outpost, but we, like every other civilised authority, do not send minor offenders to prison. But unlike you, we still believe in corporal punishment.'

Sam could hear the officer reading out a list of offences to the first of the three and asking if he agreed. The man nodded, and the officer moved on to the second.

'They are standing there proud, unshackled because no one ties down a Mineran and lives. Pat and the others will take their punishment as soldiers. It'll hurt, but this is mostly symbolic; they are tough SOB's, she more so. They will also be fined, and certain privileges will be withdrawn. Just stay calm.' He removed his arm from Sam's torso, no longer pinning it, Sam's arm and the pistol, down.

Sam looked at Apate, thin, strong and lithe at the same time. Small breasts with nipples standing proudly in the spring chill. She nodded to the officer, and he walked behind the firing line.

Sam heard the order barked out, 'Take aim!'

The rifle barrels moved a fraction as the sights were lined up with their targets.

'Fire!'

Sam was looking at Apate as the order was given. She never wavered, her eyes looking forward towards the firing line. She made no attempt to flee, the weapons made no sound, her body shook as it was battered by multiple projectiles. Four red circles appeared on her chest above her petite breasts. Thin red lines trailed downwards hardly slowing as they traversed her bosom, but petering out before they reached her shaved pubic region. The men had also been shot in the chest; their pectoral muscles showed similar damage. Sam could see the tissue around the wounds visibly changing colour and bruising.

He turned and looked across the vehicle to Reb, 'I don't understand, they should be dead.'

'I said we believe in corporal punishment, not murder Sam. They are firing tactical training rounds, simulation, er, similar to your paintball guns. These are incredibly overpowered to what you are used to, and they hurt like hell. That's the point, a real bullet hurts a hell of a lot more.' He started the engine as the second silent volley was fired; both thighs on Apate now showed aggressive welts and pseudo blood trickled down to her knees. 'They are stripped to remove rank, to remind them we are all Minerans under the uniform. We are fallible, we are mortal, and we make mistakes. As soldiers, if we lack discipline or make mistakes, it can cost lives.' Reb pulled the vehicle from the centre and drove down one of the straight roads towards the mountain.

In fact, the carbines being used were not, as Sam thought, just training weapons. The Multi-Payload Assault Rifle (MPAR) utilised a propelling force that is so small, so minute that people forgot that it existed. The force that bound all nuclei together in the atom, essentially binding the whole universe together, could be replicated and reversed. That fundamental property was first weaponised by the N'eiauc in the form of an atom disruptive ray. It literally allowed the victim's atoms to break apart. The protons, electrons and neutrons, having no cohesive force, simply dissolved. On a living entity, that was not as serene as it sounded. The weapon had limited range due to the ray's dispersal rate. It was only truly effective within a few feet of the target. The forces involved were eventually fine-tuned to repel atoms with a minimal power requirement, thus allowing for the creation of Ultimate Multiple Payload Personal Railgun.

The Universe Police used a 25mm bore automatic rifle with a half a metre length barrel, horizontal top mounted magazine and recoil stabilisers which were tuned to the payload and its velocity. Velocity and distance were automatically calculated by the computer. That could be overridden via a thumb-activated slide on the left-hand side of the non-metallic polymer based weapon. Fine-tuning for species density or armour could be adjusted via voice control. There was no muzzle flash as there was no explosion of propellants – and the payload delivery was virtually silent if used sub-sonically.

In a typical non-combative policing scenario, the round would be a 10mm metal concussive slug. It mushroomed on impact to prevent pass-through in a civilian area and then detonated within the torso.

The perfect shot was one which entered the target's chest cavity, exploded internally and liquefied the subject's internal organs with no pass-through to endanger nearby non-combatants. If the Universe Police had been called into action, circumstances had gone beyond mere policing and the objective was to shoot to kill.

In a purely military scenario, a smaller, tougher armour-piercing munition was used with similar explosive potential. Fifty rounds per magazine were allowed, plus five easily selectable bunker buster rounds which, if fired into a room, would take the whole building down.

Today the payload was an innocuous 20mm gelatine sphere with red marker dye, with the velocity set to hurt but not break the skin.

Sam put the case in the foot well and wedged it firmly with his right foot to prevent it from sliding around. 'Who did she hit?'

'One of the few people you have met so far, Timon. He's the guy you threw into the cell. He hasn't been the same since his wife died.' Seeing Sam's quizzical look he continued, 'The burnt out house that we met at, he built it. His wife and unborn child were in there when it happened. She should have returned to the home planet, but she wanted to finish her study on non-indigenous oceanic bacteria before she left. She must have been asleep at the time of the fire otherwise she'd have gotten out. They never figured out what caused it or why it burnt so fast.'

'It was a bit heartless sending me there, Reb. I'm not sure I'd be happy about it either.'

'It was a long time ago. Seventy-three years ago, in fact, Sam, and the building should have been pulled down.' He looked towards Sam to see what effect this snippet of information had on him. 'Don't look at me like that, we don't live long compared to some species. You're the ones who have a brief existence.'

They drove in silence for a few minutes as Sam tried to examine the surrounding countryside and the mountain that loomed up ahead of them. A million stupid questions filled his head as another part of his brain processed the relevant information.

'Why are we in a Toyota? Don't you have hover or flying cars and such things?'

'You have hovercraft, Sam. They make dreadful cars as they can be blown sideways. You are right, though, we do have much better transportation than this. However, as I mentioned earlier, when on a planet we try to utilise the local tech and practices as much as possible. Even in secure enclaves such as this. This isn't a Toyota, not really. We bought a second-hand cruiser and then built our own improved version. It'll never rust, the metal is much stronger, and it will run for a month on a tank of Emliton's biofuel.' Reb looked across to Sam as he changed gear and gunned the engine around the country lane. 'Before you ask, we bought the original for the registration plates. We can take this improved clone out into the world and drive around without worrying.'

'Ok, why projectile weapons? If I had previously believed in your existence, I would have expected more from you.' Sam gave a questioning look, while preventing the case from slipping from between his leg and the drive shaft hump.

'As you well know, they're simple, cheap and efficient. When you begin training, you will discover a plethora of weapons from all over the universe. Each species has its favourite method of killing one another. From weapons using various wavelengths from the light spectrum, lasers, microwaves, sound disruptors to chemical weapons, plasma, energy and projectiles. Generally, we use projectiles planet side and lasers in space. Even a military laser will eventually dissipate in space where a projectile will only stop once it hits something. If you miss the target in space, someone somewhere, maybe even a thousand years later, could get wiped out and never know what hit them.'

Reb slowed down as they drew closer to a junction. Sam found it strange that he was in a car with an alien, in a hidden secret enclave, being driven around in an alien replica of a Land Cruiser and yet they still pulled up at a give-way sign. It had all turned upside down for him and yet it was all exactly the same. He'd stumbled upon a massive life-changing secret, and yet nothing had actually changed. Life carried on around him as it always had.

CHAPTER 10

The rest of the drive took less than twenty minutes, most of which Sam sat quietly as he tried to digest everything that he had seen in the last twenty-four hours. He was deep in thought as he felt the car pull to a stop and heard the ratchet as Reb applied the hand brake. He looked ahead and saw a large concrete entrance reminiscent to the opening at Cheyenne Mountain, not that he had been there, but he'd seen it on Stargate. He chuckled to himself as he disembarked, grabbing the case as he did so.

'The road goes further in, but we might as well walk from here as you will get a better look at our operation.' Reb didn't wait for a reply and proceeded to walk towards the dark, impending opening. He bent down and picked up a small rock from the verge. Shouting over his shoulder, 'I know you have had a lot to take in Sam, but you are the one who broke into our warehouse. You were never in any danger from us, though. We have had you under surveillance for weeks, and we could have wiped your short-term memory with a mere drop in your food. You have been led to this point, nearly everything that has happened was planned, a gradual path of enlightenment to recruit you. Well, everything except for Urser, of course.' He stopped and looked back as Sam caught up.

'Why did Urser target me? Have you figured out how he knew I was going to be there?'

'I don't know is the answer to both. Nik's findings are worrisome, to say the least. We have no idea who, why or when it was instigated. The perpetrator could even be an ally at this moment in time with no intention or inclination of future betrayal. In time the mystery will unfold. Time being the operative word here.'

Turning, they both walked through the tunnel's opening, Sam's eyes slowly adjusting to the dark, unlit interior. He knew it would take about half an hour for his eyes to fully adjust to night vision and he could only hope he didn't fall over something in the meantime. It was all down to the cones and rods in his eyes; the outer cones being the ones responsible for his low light vision, an evolutionary masterpiece even if it was strongest on the periphery.

They had only walked a dozen or so feet into the entrance when a long dotted line of automated lights blinked into existence. The tunnel had a gradual downward slope. Sam approximated it to be a gradient of one in twenty, losing one foot for every twenty travelled. The walls and ceiling were clean and dry, painted light green to head height and bright white from then on. The tunnel was big enough for two double decker buses to travel side by side and gradually curved to the left and down, leaving a visible length of half a mile. Road and walkways were clearly marked with a gantry system high up for light and ventilation maintenance. There were a handful of electric carts along the side walls, their charging bays distinguished by bright yellow boxes.

'It doesn't seem very busy,' Sam commented as he subconsciously orientated towards a predefined pathway, even though there was no traffic.

'The barrels you are so concerned about will appear ahead of us in about ten minutes. From there we will follow them for fifteen minutes till the end point. You have my guarantee that you will not be displeased with the outcome.'

'So what did you want to talk about, Reb? The scenery isn't much to look at, you must have something you need to say.'

'Sam, I have already told you that we are a quasi-military police force tasked with protecting certain areas and re-enforcing local police forces. Primarily we need a native born, someone from earth to help us investigate off-world incursions on your planet. Someone who knows how your world and cultures work, someone who will be ignored by off-worlders. Their security will show you rightly as human, and they will assume that you are ignorant of their presence. You can go where we can't. As I told you, your authorities know of the alien presence, and many are aligned to different factions. They turn a blind eye, thinking they are gaining something, never realising the nefarious nature of such alliances.' Reb carried on walking and talking as if this conversation was an everyday occurrence.

'Across the universe, normal police are good at enforcing the law-abiding citizens, but they are not trained or equipped to deal with hardcore armed criminals. We also get called into these situations. When No Go zones appear in towns and cities, we clean them out. If, when you have seen what we are doing here, and...' He paused. 'Well, you will not be able to deny my origin and what I have said.' He stopped and looked at Sam. In the silence, Sam could hear a faint rumble of machinery and conveyors. 'I have been honest with you, and we do want to recruit you, but it's your choice. Sign up and you will have an adventure of a lifetime; everything your sci-fi writers have ever thought up has happened somewhere out there. You can be part of it, or you can go back to your old life. Oh, we looked into your friend's business by the way. Besides fronting for MI5, he seems legitimate enough, and he pays the regular employees well, files his tax returns on time and he's faithful to his wife. You could do worse, but you have the opportunity to do so much better.'

'Tell me more about your judicial system. So far, all I have seen is you torturing your own people. They're so afraid they stand there waiting to be punished.'

'Sam, stop being childish. You know as well as I do that your system does not work. Your prisons are overcrowded, most criminals get away with a verbal telling off by the courts and sent on their merry way to continue. People have lost faith. Your society is one step away from snapping and then you will have vigilantes roaming the streets. In fact, it's happening now, only it's hushed-over to prevent further take- up by the populace. Our system categorises criminal acts in five levels. Levels one to two can be anything from spitting in the streets to minor assault. These are all dealt with locally and corporal punishment and fines administered accordingly. All proceeds from any fines go to local projects or charities. The governing body of the areas are not allowed to use or keep said proceeds. This maintains the courts' impartiality and prevents accusations of stealth taxation via fines.'

'What type of corporal punishment is used? I can't imagine shooting someone is acceptable elsewhere.'

'It's species dependant of course, but nothing that leaves a permanent injury can be used. Lashing of miscreants is common throughout as it is quick, cheap and effective. It is always public, as to visually deter others.'

'Ok, go on.'

'Level three is for crimes such as burglary, vehicle theft and tax evasion. Each instance will earn the criminal half a bar, a public lashing and time in a penal system, similar to the one that Urser is at now.'

'A bar being part of the triangle tattoo you mentioned earlier?'

'Exactly, the triptych. Gaining a full bar also loses you the right to reproduce.' After an enquiring look for further questions he continued. 'Level four is for more serious crime: the supply of narcotics, aggravated assault and brandishing a weapon at any member of police, pyro brigade etcetera. This will get you a full bar and time in the PeCo, sorry penal colony. All penal systems tend to be located on the less desirable worlds. Ones with a heavier gravity are preferable as it tires the inmates out quicker. Level five in the criminal system is for things like treason, premeditated murder and using a weapon against any member of the police or other forces. You only have three choices, you either choose a humane death, solitary life imprisonment on a terraforming planet or a life term in the Shock Troopers which has an average life expectancy of thirteen years. That's about it. Pretty simple – after several millennia of civilisation, the answer to nearly everything is to keep it cheap and simple.'

Continuing on in silence, Sam once again mulled over the large volumes of unbelievable information he was being presented with. Amongst his thoughts, he realised he could feel the vibration of machinery through the floor. Looking ahead he could see the opening of another tunnel becoming visible around the curvature. As they continued to descend what Sam could only imagine as a large lazy downward spiral, the promised conveyor system became apparent and began to run parallel with the road.

'There's no echo. We should have heard the reverberations from the entrance.'

'It's the paint,' answered Reb. 'It's been formulated for noisy environments so it absorbs most of the sound.'

A long stream of barrels trundled along a raised platform emerging from a side tunnel. Sam was aghast at the quantity. Each one contained toxic waste of some kind, any one of which could leak into the water table, polluting the area for miles around.

Sam felt his patience wear thin. 'Are you immune to the toxicity of one of those leaks?' he asked vehemently.

'No, I'm flesh and blood, same as you Sam. You saw the protective suits, so you know we are not immune. But they won't ever leak, rust or break. The spraying process you witnessed is a molecular compound that bonds with the metal to form an impregnable outer coating. Protecting the environment is part of our ethos and way of life. Besides, our history shows a plethora of civilisations that withered away due to them destroying their home planet. You're teetering on the edge now. Without our clandestine intervention, you'd have passed the point of no return decades ago.' Reb stopped to look Sam in the eyes. 'Did you know that in the Pacific Ocean there is an area called the Pacific trash vortex? A patch of debris and plastic flotsam larger than the state of Texas. Not only is the marine life being entangled and killed by it but the plastic breaks down, saturating the area for miles around with toxic polymers that are ingested, endangering every species in this field. So don't pull the environmental card on me. You are the monsters here, you all turn a blind eye and pretend it has nothing to do with you, and someone else will fix it. Your industries don't care, and your governments kowtow down to them, begging bowls in hand. Your planet is only focused on profit and power.' Anger and frustration tempered Reb's voice, portraying a hard side of Reb that Sam hadn't previously seen.

'But you're apparently storing them below ground, even with your coating you are only delaying the inevitable.'

'Are we? Would you like to put a wager on it? After everything you have been told you are still thinking two-dimensionally.'

'First off, do you realise you sound like an extra from Star Trek? I honestly thought you were going to mention M-Class planets earlier and now the Spock, Khan quote. Do you really want me to take you seriously?'

Reb laughed. 'Ah, we do love your TV, but I am more of a fan of Firefly myself, it's a bit more true-to-life. Even in space the simple low-tech answer is often the most effective and thus more commonly used.' Still chuckling to himself, he continued, 'I certainly wouldn't want a door that shushed me every time it opened and closed.'

'Funny,' a dejected Sam replied. 'If we are going down, you are either storing them or dropping them down a very deep shaft. It's not warm enough for there to be a lava pit down there and we would have smelt the sulphur.'

'Well firstly, it'd be a magma pit as we are below ground and lava is above. It is what spills out of a volcano. Secondly, no, we are not doing either of those things. You will have to wait a few minutes. The answer is just around the corner.'

They were walking alongside the conveyor now; the tunnel had widened to accommodate the extra machinery. Further along, Sam could see rows of large stacked cubes. They were polished bright, reflecting the light from overhead. Sam cast a questioning glance at Reb.

'Would it make sense if I said they are a by-product of the process? To be precise, they are two-metre tall cubes of solid steel or eight cubic metres of steel weighing over sixty-two thousand kilogrammes each. Does that help?' The sarcastic tone failed to mask Reb's amusement at Sam's quandary.

Sam touched one of the cubes as he walked by. The sides were perfectly smooth, and he couldn't see the top as it was above his head height. The edges and corners were rounded, giving the cubes a look of gigantic dice.

A subdued glow was faintly visible from the end of the conveyor. Sam calculated it to be a quarter of a mile away. He didn't bother to figure out how many barrels were passing him on the conveyor. A steady stream of them, spaced six feet apart, were travelling lengthways, slightly faster than the pace they were walking at. They disappeared ahead, near the glow. Sam could not make out what was happening, it all seemed to be occurring in shadows, which didn't make sense as it was also glowing.

He picked up his pace a bit, subconsciously eager to solve the mystery. 'Do I need to wear a suit or anything?' he enquired.

'No, but do not and I stress DO NOT touch anything. In fact, put your hands in your pockets when you get there,' Reb replied cryptically.

He could feel the heat; it was definitely getting warmer as he drew nearer to the glow. The air had the feel of a smithy he had once visited. It had a perceptible ferrous taste. He could partially see the end wall of the tunnel thirty or forty feet behind the glow, but something large and dark was obscuring the view.

The conveyor ended suddenly with a short downward section. The barrels seemed to enter a dark cave. Bastards, he thought, they are dumping the drums, after all, that bullshit and holier-than-thou crap he had been fed. The bright glow prevented him from seeing into the new cave or tunnel entrance. It seemed to be a set of ultra-bright strip lights. In his haste, Sam had gotten ahead of Reb at this point; he looked back with anger in his eyes.

'You go ahead, I'll catch you up. For your own safety, please do not go up the gantry steps or go into the red zone.'

Sam didn't realise it, but he had broken out into a small jog as he strained to see clearly what was happening. What seemed to be a tunnel entrance from further back must be the opening of a large twenty-foot diameter pipe, whose opening was facing directly at him as the opening was floating in the centre of the tunnel.

He could see the barrels rise to the top of the conveyor's apex and then descend, lost in the illumination from the bright strip lights. At thirty feet, his assumptions fell apart. He could see that the glowing strip lights were, in fact, a constant stream of bright luminescent liquid flowing into a grill in the floor. 'None of this makes sense,' he muttered to himself. 'If the liquid was the toxic waste, what's the pipe for?' He looked back at Reb. 'I don't understand, you're just dumping it all into the ground, but what's the pipe for?'

'Look closer, Sam, you not allowing yourself to see the truth.'

Sam paused at the railings which separated the danger

zone from the walkway with the aid of red markings on the floor, defining a twenty-foot radius from the illicit dumping area. The whole area was brightly lit. The liquid wasn't luminescent. It was white hot. He could feel the heat searing his skin even from this distance. The pipe was blacker than night. It was void of any reflection from the incandescent liquid that was pouring down. The barrels moved along the conveyor, and they should have fallen into the centre of the dark yearning chasm and rolled away. Instead, they seemed to hit a solid barrier. Where the metal met the beginning of the opening, it instantly became molten liquid, running down across an invisible surface and into the grate in the floor.

Sam walked around the railing to try and see the process from the side. He didn't hear Reb as he eventually ambled alongside him. There was no pipe, there was no nothing. From his vantage point at the side, the barrels stopped their descent from the conveyor in mid-air. The metal simply melted as if it were merely chocolate touching a white hot skillet. It ran down and back towards the direction of the conveyor. A river of molten metal floated in the air as if it were on top of an invisible thin sheet of glass that was set at a thirty-five-degree angle. Sam walked further round to see if he could make sense of what he was seeing. All he could see was blackness, a huge disc of blackness.

'I don't understand.'

'My ancient ancestors with their primitive minds called it "Dia Kuklos" because they could go through the circle. This is the cause of distortion here in Minera. This is what we guard, keep secret and safe. This is our primary duty.'

'So is this a black hole? Shouldn't all of our solar system be sucked into it?'

'No, you're not seeing what is in front of you, Sam. Come back to the front and watch.' Sam and Reb walked back along the railing to view the barrels landing on the Dia Kuklos.

'Think back to the balloon model we discussed. If two distortions happened to touch each other, they'd perforate the fabric of space and link together. You can literally step through one side to the other. Your scientists theorise about this and commonly call them wormholes. There's no tunnel connecting them. Both openings occupy the same space at the same time. They have many names in different cultures throughout the universe such as spatial apertures or perforations, portals, Quantum eyelets, interstices.'

He looked at Sam, beaming. 'Cool, eh? So we are using this cosmic abnormality to dump your toxic waste. Just not where you thought. The metal can't get through the surface tension. The reaction is so volatile that it melts upon contact. We use this to allow the waste to escape and flow through while collecting the metal for recycling.'

'So you're saying I could step through to wherever you are dumping this stuff?'

'Well, you could step through, Sam, but you wouldn't last very long. The other side is in a fixed position near a star you call Canopus. Over the course of a year or so, the waste is gently drawn in by its gravitational pull and destroyed. The aperture itself is black because neither side opens facing the star. If you could pop your head through and look to the right...' Reb shrugged and put his hand on Sam's shoulder. 'I was hoping to have thought of something witty to say by now, but, there you go. What else can I do to prove to you we are the good guys?' He handed Sam the small stone from his pocket. 'Go ahead and toss it in, watch it float away. Do it from the other side to get a better view.'

Sam walked to the rear side of the aperture and gently, with an underarm throw, tossed the stone through the portal. It physically slowed as it passed through what Reb had called the surface tension. It carried on into the darkness with its left-hand side clearly visible as it was being illuminated by the unseen sun.

'Why are you guarding these, why the secrecy?'

'Why? Well, that's a long story, but I'll keep it brief. My race evolved on planet Minera long before the Overseer arrived. As our population spread over the planet, legend says they found a portal and called it "Dia Kuklos". It happened in the midst of the harshest winter in history. My primitive ancestors found a window to a sunny world; it saved thousands of lives. They sought refuge through it and others harvested food and brought it back. Over the centuries, we eventually learnt how to detect the distortions in the fabric of space and found thirty more on our planet. Because of the nature of their original creation, these portals were always located within spatial distortions like Minera, making them difficult to find unless you know what to look for. Not all distortions contained a portal and many, being like this one, open into empty space, or hundreds of feet above the ground. As our technology evolved and resources dwindled, we abused these portals to other worlds to carry out raids and wage war.'

'We discovered one portal close to a black hole. The conflicting forces waged between the portal, and the event horizon of the black hole made it jittery. The other end wasn't permanently fixed. It sporadically lashed across the universe, momentarily setting on other portals. We learnt how to manipulate it with gravitational and spatial distorting fields. We could lock onto other portals within its original range. It is, to this date, the only one we know of with this ability. History says we were ruthless, relentless and barbaric. To the unwary, we came out of nowhere. Whole armies massed secretly in the distorted areas, unseen by the local population. It was an era of terror that we waged covertly over the universe and a shame we still carry. The Overseer stopped this. Somehow he changed the surface tension on all of the portals. Nothing but light passed through; they became useless windows. In one fell swoop, he had isolated us. We had no long distance space travel technology as we had never needed to develop it. Our planet was over populated, and resources strained. He gave us an ultimatum, either we sign up and with our knowledge locate these portals throughout the universe and guard them against further abuse or he would cause our extinction.'

'The elders in their vanity would not bow down to an unknown enemy, and millions died as ruthless factions fought amongst each other for the dwindling resources. After 225 years of planet-bound war, they realised no children had been born. We had been sterilised. The last generation to be born were now in charge, and the war machine had fizzled out long ago. The remaining populace had reverted to a simpler way of life. The preservation of life and the recovery of our planet became almost a religion. It was a hybrid of high technology and ecological, environmentally friendly living. On the eve of 250 years, the Overseer spoke again. The message was clear: police the portals for him or die out. The rest is history, as they say, they capitulated, and we have served him ever since. The Overseer returned to us the ability to reproduce and the use of the portals, though he has never allowed any metal to pass through since.'

'Well, that's not what I expected. I don't know what to say.'

'There is nothing to say, but you can see a similarity between our chequered history and how your civilisation's developing. It took a long time for our planet to recover from our greed and negligence.' Reb ushered Sam back around with his arms. 'We try to keep the portals secret to make our life easier. There are only a few races out there that are partially aware of them. For some they are a thing of myth and legend, magic gateways to other worlds, but nothing more.'

Sam subconsciously switched the case to his left arm as he walked back around.

'The process,' swinging his arm at the conveyor, 'should end in a few minutes, then we have a few people to see.'

CHAPTER 11

Reb's head flew up as something caught his attention. He quickly moved himself in front of Sam, hugging and pushing his head down at the same time. The crack of assault rifles reverberated across the cavernous tunnel, regardless of the sound- dampening paint. Sam felt the impact of seven or eight bullets as they struck Reb in the back. The shudder of the impact passed through to him as Sam took on the full weight of his body.

Other bullets impacted all around him, causing shards of concrete splinters to fly all around. He grabbed what was left of Reb, and using his body as a shield, moved behind one of the huge steel blocks that were scattered around. 'Shit!' he expelled, as he tried to lower Reb to the ground with some reverence. He had, after all, sacrificed his life for Sam.

'Oh God, that hurt. Bob, what the hell's going on? Who are they and where did they come from?' Reb shouted to no one in particular.

'What the fu—' He was cut short as Reb waved his arm for silence and stuck his finger in his ear.

Kneeling down, Reb popped his head around the corner of the block and just as quickly drew his weapon, firing off a short burst with a surreal, silent 'pfft' as the muzzle flashed brightly. 'Should slow them down for a second.'

Sam looked at Reb's back. The long overcoat that he always wore and trousers were pockmarked with bright, shiny metal bullets. Each one held what appeared to be a gel that had solidified upon impact. Without thinking, Sam brushed a squashed bullet off the coat and watched as the area reset to a flexible fabric.

'What do you mean there is no one else here, I can bloody well see them.' He indicated to Sam to take up a position on the other side of the block. Drawing his Glock, he did so.

Peering around, he saw three massive brutes taking cover from Reb's fire. In the distance, he could make out a group of others rushing around the curve of the tunnel. 'There's more on the way, at least another eight,' he shouted to Reb.

'Bob, we need backup now! What, we haven't got ten minutes. How did they get through? What do you mean there are only sheep in the tunnels, do they fucking look like sheep to you? I don't care what the computer says. Get me some backup, now!'

Upon seeing their comrades closing the half-mile gap, two of which must have been an advanced scouting party, they leapt out with bravado, firing their carbines on full auto as they dashed to the next steel block. Both Reb and Sam took this opportunity to fire into the face of an inaccurate but just as deadly fusillade. Both running assailants took the explosive small arms fire to their chests. Sam was silently impressed at the reduced recoil and improved accuracy of his cloned weapon. He was less impressed at the supposedly improved munitions. 'I thought you said these were explosive rounds,' he angrily shouted towards Reb.

'They are, one of these should take down a rhino.' The aggressors each had four or five gaping wounds to the chest. The flesh was hanging off them, yet they still continued on. 'Aim for the head.' Reb's next bullet took the man down with a crimson burst of colour that looked surreal as it splattered across the huge silvery dice behind. Sam grazed the head of his target just before he managed to gain the safety of another cube.

Inaccurate rifle fire suddenly pockmarked the cubes around Sam and Reb. Two of the approaching squad had climbed upon the metal blocks to offer a steady stream of suppressive covering fire. The main squad were approaching fast. Sam ejected the empty magazine. The prognosis for the next five minutes was not good. Pistols against rifles. They already had the advantage, never mind the superior numbers and the fact that Sam had hit the assailant at least five times, and he was still fighting. He was down to thirty rounds in two magazines. 'Make them count,' he said to no one in particular.

The barrels continued to trundle on above them, the sound of the conveyor muffled by the clack of metal hitting metal as bullets flew through the air. The last barrel was in sight, at this rate of progress, it would be processed in less than a minute.

'Bob, I need you to stop the conveyor and divert the portal. We need to get out of here.' He looked up as the rumble ceased. 'Put the station on alert and tell them we are coming in hot. Get ready to reset the portal as soon as we pass through.'

The main force gathered just outside the pistol's effective range, the controlled shots from Reb that were striking them were more of an annoyance rather than a terminal kiss of lead. They didn't seem worried about waiting an extra few minutes to allow their quarry to deplete the limited cache of ammunition.

'Who are they?' Sam asked in a brief lull as they regrouped for the next onslaught.

'Never seen them before, bipedal, humanoid and ugly. Although unlike you, they seem to be pretty immune to your primitive weapons,' indicating his pistol, 'even with our modifications. They must have an incredible muscle density and bone structure. Clearly, our shots are not getting past the rib cage. Bob is arranging for the portal to relocate to the station. Strip off now and when I say, run up the gantry and jump through slowly. The surface reacts badly to velocity. Oh, and try to hit the event horizon parallel. Sam, it's going to hurt. You've got pins in your leg.'

Sam looked at the portal. It looked even blacker now that the heated metal was no longer pouring down its front. He looked at the cubes, suddenly realising that these were formed from the leftover metal from the process. Then he looked down at his right leg. 'Shit!' He stripped off as quickly as he could. For some reason being naked in the midst of a firefight made him feel extra vulnerable. He fired off a few shots to make himself feel better and managed to take out the previously wounded scouts with a satisfying headshot.

He was grateful that the metal cubes were made from a soft steel. The bullets mushroomed into them rather than spraying him with shrapnel or ricocheting about wildly.

'What do you mean you can't divert, you can't be blocked out?' As the heated discussion progressed, the black portal visibly shimmered with a variety of dark hues. Reb managed to catch the third scout in the head. His body crumpled to the ground, blood and cranial matter flowing onto the concrete floor.

'The others are massing for a charge, get ready. Bob, how are we doing with the portal? What? No, it's still black, I don't know.' Reb used his leg to quickly flick the plastic case that Sam had dropped behind the cube, just in time to avoid the next heavy salvo. 'They're coming.'

Sam braved the volley of bullets. He knew his luck couldn't last much longer. He was already more exposed than he wanted to be, firing right-handed around a left-hand corner and now he was nude. He managed three head shots with the careful and calm precision that a trained soldier got from knowing that you were certainly going to die, and there was nothing you could do but seek pre-revenge.

'Sorry, Doc,' Reb said as he took out three of the four glass containers and threw them towards the charging brutes. They crashed onto the tunnel floor ahead of them. Reb had already wrapped a cloth around the fourth canister while Sam was preoccupied firing and now lit it with a hand lighter and threw.

The combustible vapour that now permeated the tunnel ignited with a whump long before the projectile crashed onto the floor, sending its liquid fire in all directions. The fire burnt fiercely with tall flames, but with little to consume it within the tunnel, it would only last a short while.

Reb looked across to Sam with a grin, only to see him leaning heavily onto the cube. Sam's face was ashen, and blood was seeping down his torso from wounds on both sides of his right shoulder. An arrow-like projectile had skewered him to the cube. Thankfully it had not passed through Sam completely as the vicious looking finned tail would have caused horrendous tissue trauma. Most alarmingly, the projectile must have come from the portal.

'Bob, what the hell's happening?' He moved towards Sam to assess the situation as the portal shimmered to settle, showing a steel gantry leading down to a room full of hostile-looking soldiers. Thankfully they wore Mineran uniforms. 'Sam, I'm going to pull you free of the cube, we need to leave the arrow in to staunch the flow.'

'Yeah, sorry,' Sam replied groggily. 'Yeah, ok.' He looked down at the arrow. 'It's too high to have pierced the lung. But stupidly I nearly blacked out as I hit my head on the block.' He broke out into a traumatic, shock-induced laugh. 'I've been shot with a bloody arrow in a gun fight. If this is how you treat your friends I'd hate to see you on a date.'

'Someone knows our history; this is a ceramic version of an ancestral arrow. If those fins feel any pressure from penetration, the whole back end will suddenly resemble an angry porcupine. It gets real messy.' Sam blanched as Reb pulled the arrow and him with equal force. Sam groaned as he did so. 'We need to go now. The portal is open. Go in forwards and try not to fall backwards onto the arrow.' He pulled a small hood from inside of his coat, a quick, practiced action of fingering a tiny hoop in the back of his collar, stretching and releasing onto his forehead. It shrank to cling to the shape of his head.

Reb pushed Sam ahead as he fired off the rest of his magazine, dumped the gun and followed, covering Sam with his own body as he did so. As they ran up the gantry, bullets whipped all around. He lost count of how many hit him, his reactive body armour preventing penetration and spreading the force of the blow over a larger area. It was like being repeatedly punched, each one taking its toll on his body. He took two large blows to the head, dazing him instantly, his legs and body working independently of his consciousness to get him out of danger.

Reb was at the Dia Kuklos shortly after Sam. As he proceeded to step through, the area ahead of him suddenly splattered with blood and white hot metal as Sam's body was ripped apart from the inside. Reb managed to twist in time to miss the white hot liquid metal from Sam's leg pins. What worried him the most was the small piece of metal streaming down the portal surface at head height. He could see blood! Lots of blood.

CHAPTER 12

Sam could feel the air move around him as bullets whisked past. He knew Reb was covering his retreat and that he must be taking hits. Pumped up on adrenalin, Sam raced up the gantry towards the Dia Kuklos. Part of his mind found it funny that he was running nude towards an alien Dia Kuklos to another world full of aliens and he was making his debut with his manhood swinging about and a 16-inch arrow in his shoulder. 'You don't see this in the movies,' Sam groaned to himself as the jostling shaft sent a cascading wave of pain from his shoulder down throughout his body.

He was at the top and facing the angled surface of the Dia Kuklos. He certainly couldn't jump through feet first, as the metal pins would burn up his body. It would have been better to come at it from the other side where the angle would work in his favour, but there was no time for that. He leant forward and tried to hit the surface of the Dia Kuklos in a falling walk, turning his head at the last second to look back to see Reb. Reb's face was grim but had a look of determination. Suddenly Reb's head violently jerked forward as if he was performing a violent Glasgow Kiss and Sam realised he had just taken a shot to the back of his head. Not having seen Reb apply the hood he thought him surely dead. At that instant, Sam's face exploded!

He had utterly overlooked a forgotten amalgamation of mercury, silver, tin and copper, which instantly heated up to a liquid state. The sudden increase in size shattered the bottom molar that it had previously protected. The superheated liquid destroyed and cauterised flesh at the same time. Here was where Sam's luck ran out as the molten metal had to pass through from right to left. If only he had looked the other way! Heat seared and burnt his mouth and throat, and the super-heated air made its way into his lungs, seriously charring the interior surface and making it impossible for him to breathe. The molten metal burnt its way through Sam's tongue and lower jaw until it finally escaped through the left check. A fraction of a second later, seven micro pins burnt through his fibula, tibia and calf muscle.

Sam fell into a pair of outstretched arms. He couldn't breathe as the nerves in his lungs screamed that they were on fire. It felt like most of his face was missing and in the haze of pain he was sure he saw part of his tongue fall to the floor. For some reason, the last thought that ran through his mind was 'mind the porcupine.' Then blackness enveloped him and the pain went away.

~*~

The Station Doctor was waiting for Reb and the human to appear through the still dark Dia Kuklos. He was accompanied by twenty heavily armed, albeit, frustrated Minerans in full battle armour and non-metallic carbines. He was as surprised as they were that Bob had instructed them not to dash through the Dia Kuklos once it was redirected. They were to attend to Reb and Sam as they appeared and defend the station with extreme prejudice. As soon as the alert went out, they had mustered here and watched the enthralling developments in the tunnels via the almost live feed on the surveillance screen. Once a Dia Kuklos connection was made it would catch up.

The new foe was intriguing. He had studied and dissected examples of most of the life forms which had joined the ISPAW and he didn't recognise these. The others watching the screen wouldn't have noticed, of course. The evolution of these bipeds had traded high pain thresholds, alongside the enhanced skeletal and muscular features which offered greater protection to physical impact. However, it was at the cost of flexibility, manoeuvrability and from the looks of it, intellect. He didn't think this was a natural process as the brutes were poorly kitted out for their physical size. An invading army would come prepared, whereas these had oversized hands that struggled to handle the weapons and the trigger guards were missing to accommodate the fat fingers. The doc could only assume their evolution had recently been expedited in a lab on earth, ergo these were modified Homo sapiens. 'I do hope you can save one of these, Sergeant, they are a physical anomaly,' he said to the burly squad leader who stood with a pensive look. No one likes to be ordered to leave a friend in the line of fire.

'I can't promise that, Doc,' he drawled. 'Bob thinks they will rush through the Dia Kuklos, so as soon as Reb gets through he'll switch it back to open in space. Captain Sophus is currently engaging a small force at the tunnel entrance.' Thankfully he had put the men on alert after the first incursion and had manned SUVs on patrol. 'I hope he keeps one alive for questioning.' He tilted his hand to show the tablet screen showing a feed taken from the tunnel entrance. The patrolling Minerans from the enclave were not restricted to using local weapons, and with their superior firepower, they were overwhelming the rear guard. At the forefront was a ferocious and proficient naked female, who had arrived shortly after the battle began on an all-terrain motorbike. Her whole body seemed to be pockmarked with bruises.

'I'm not that familiar with your tactical procedure and operations, Sergeant, but is that a standard tactic?'

'No, that's Apate, Doc. I have no idea and nor will I be foolish enough to enquire.' He raised an eyebrow at the doctor. 'Although it does seem to bewilder the enemy, maybe that's her tactic.' They continued to watch as she methodically decimated the enemy by taking calm and precise aim amidst the volley of fire aimed towards her. The other Minerans supplied huge volumes of covering fire, and moved up alongside their heroic angel of death towards the entrance. She could be seen barking a warning to her comrades, who quickly dove into cover. She fired a bunker buster round into the entrance and the vehicles evaporated into a deadly cloud of shrapnel. She never slowed her advance into the now dust, and smoke enshrouded passage. Using the heat sensing sight, she continued to lay down a deadly barrage of fire.

The doctor and the sergeant watched with fascination as she approached the remaining foe. 'I believe she has an ulterior motive. Apparently, she really likes him.' The doctor was looking at the sergeant but he could not read any expression on his face. 'He'd have my sympathy, but at this moment I feel sorry for those two brutes. A woman vexed is a heinous beast at the best of times – and she has an MPAR carbine.' He winced. 'Ooh, that's got to hurt.'

The doctor, who was far older than any of the other Minerans, had a passion for all things historic. He, like everyone else there, had been listening to Reb's audio feed as the station technicians overlaid the signal with the video feed. Seeing a replica of the ancient Spica Sagitta in action intrigued him. Or, as it was more commonly and incorrectly called, "The Arrow of a Thousand Needles". Shame it didn't activate as the results would have been spectacular to watch.

Clearly, someone was using it to taunt the Minerans. This attack was showing they knew about Mineran history, the Dia Kuklos and how to hijack and divert them. He couldn't fathom if it was the same adversary that sent Urser, as there was not enough information to go on. He did like a good puzzle, and things had been too quiet for the last hundred years or so. There should be interesting times ahead and this puny human, for some reason, was in the middle of it all.

As he watched the feed of Reb pulling Sam free from the cube, the Dia Kuklos shimmered. The Doctor realised the enemy's hubris and gesturing may well have saved Sam's life.

Thinking ahead, he could play out the bolt's effectiveness on some of the cadavers, knowing that he'd be asked to examine and perform the post-mortems. If this human didn't survive, he could inadvertently nudge the arrow a little and watch it spring spectacularly to life.

Via the screen, he could see Sam and Reb running up the gantry. Their heads were coming into view through the Dia Kuklos itself. The fire had given them a few scant seconds of relief, the brutish forward stampede had stalled, and one went down from Reb's parting shots as he ran for the platform. Bullets impacted with the Dia Kuklos' surface tension, instantly melting and slowly dribbling downwards causing further obstacles for Reb and Sam to avoid. He walked closer to the Dia Kuklos to catch Sam as he passed through. A gurney and nurse were waiting close by.

CHAPTER 19

The huge cadaver lay on a cold metal table. The doctor had thoughtfully cleaned the area up prior to his guests arriving, including hosing down the blood sluice, covering any organs he had removed and, more importantly, masking the smell of the recent autopsy.

Three figures walked into the white, cold, examination room; they were dwarfed by the overly tall door – one of the concessions the station designers had given the doctor while it was being updated a few years ago. All of the major doors were 3.2 metres tall to allow him unhindered access.

The doctor was sitting on a comfortable office chair next to the table to accommodate the diminutive forms of the Minerans. 'Thank you for popping in on short notice, I know you have a lot of investigating to do regarding the recent events. I thought you would like to hear my preliminary findings.'

'What have you got for us, Doc?' Captain Sophus said. He had taken on the role of Acting Commander on the station for the duration of the conflict, as Major Hypatia was unfortunately away on the home world. The second in command, Lieutenant Kallistrate, was not present. A shame really, as her long hair and her distinct scent made her easy to identify. They all looked so similar. The uniform made it easier as it had their ID numbers emblazoned on the breast. Thank the great divinity that they smelt so much. He would never be able to tell them apart otherwise. Not that he would ever tell them that.

'As you can see, gentlemen,' he said, holding his hand up towards the body. 'This is the finest example of evolutive and genetic engineering I've ever seen. I have found this truly stimulating, to say the least.' Realising he was coming across with too much zeal, he countered with, 'Much more interesting than repairing training wounds on your men, Captain.'

'Tell us what you have found, Doc, we are very busy at the moment and have no time to lose. Kallistrate will not be joining us as I have instructed her to carry on investigating how someone hijacked, albeit temporarily, the Dia Kuklos. As you are aware, this station was built around the only known divertible Dia Kuklos.'

The doctor nodded in appreciation of the explanation. 'These soldiers are definitely of human origin, and there is no evidence in the blood and bone analysis to indicate that they have ever been off-world. You wouldn't know it by the look of this poor fellow, but he is only six months old.' He looked at the trio for a reaction. Not finding one, he carried on. 'There are none of the usual clone indicators present and upon closer inspection, none of the bodies, whilst very similar, conform with each other. They also have a belly button. My guess would be that he started life as a human baby and ended up as a prototype of a genetic engineer soldier.'

'Prototype?' Reb enquired.

'Of the twelve bodies I have examined, I have noted four variations to the genetic alterations. They are, in truth, only using rudimentary genetic techniques, but in collaboration with evolutive serums and the rapid reproductive and growth rate of the humans.' He spread his arms. 'Well, you get something like this. Of course, they have altered the skin, muscle and bone density, there are even more ribs. You might note, Reb, that none of your little toy gun bullets penetrated past the ribs. The blood coagulates much quicker to prevent rapid blood loss and the heart, with its cardiovascular system, is designed to compensate for the increased viscosity.' He pulled a dark red heart from under a white towel. 'See? This is four times the size it should be.'

The three men, all of whom were combat veterans, didn't bat an eyelid at the site of the heart thrust under their noses.

'Is there anything else pertinent to the investigation, Doc?' the captain said with a hint of impatience.

'As you discovered when you tried to interrogate the one Apate captured, they have no tongue. Scarring shows that it was removed early in the process, I'd say five months ago, but the accelerated growth makes it hard to pin down an exact time. Shame she shot his arms off, as having gone back to the video feeds you can clearly see commands being exchanged with hand gestures. Maybe some form of sign language?' Looking directly at the captain, 'Did he really charge at her with no arms?'

'Until she shot one of his legs off. Interestingly none of them responded to pain in the way one would expect. The footage clearly shows that, no pun intended,' droned the captain. 'They showed a concern to only live long enough to finish the mission. We are assuming that they are connected with the Dia Kuklos hijack, but we have no firm foundation for that assumption. They clearly had little understanding of the Dia Kuklos as they continued to run through after Bob reset it to Canopus. They didn't know enough to drop any metal carried.'

'That fits with my prognosis of limited intellect, which is mainly based on watching the feed as there is nothing detrimental or missing in the brain itself. I would say this is a symptom of using the prototypes before they were fully developed. Did you notice they were ill equipped for their size?' He didn't wait for an answer. 'Another indication these amazing specimens were used ahead of schedule.'

'They're abominations, Doc, and the people behind this must pay,' the sergeant blurted out.

'Quite right, Sergeant,' the captain interceded, placing a calming hand on the sergeant's shoulder. 'Please continue, Doctor.'

'Correct me if I am wrong, Doc, but what you are saying is someone is experimenting on human babies to breed a formidable soldier in six months?' Reb asked before the doctor could continue.

Holding up a small appendage on the corpse, the doctor continued. 'Let's say nine months for full maturity, the testes haven't dropped yet, and there are a few other indicators. Yes, some nefarious and very wealthy organisation is performing illegal procedures on the male offspring of an unaligned world. I will catalogue the list of illicit medical procedures, but as you will have realised any one of them gives you an extreme prejudice warrant to act.'

'Thank you, Doc. Please let me recap to make sure I have got it right. It takes nine months to grow a full soldier who can withstand massive amounts of physical trauma, who is not afraid to die and as yet has an undetermined intellect.' Putting his hand up to silence the doctor, he continued. 'Not only do we have a duty to terminate this heinous atrocity on Earth, but we also have some unknown assailant breeding a secret army and a traitor in our midst,' the captain finished.

'I cannot comment on your traitor, Captain, but this is rather clever, actually. There are not many bipedal races that can breed as prolifically as the humans. They are unaware of the greater picture around them and are unable to defend themselves. Practically imbeciles by modern standards and they are genetically unadulterated. The perfect laboratory rat.'

'Doc, your coldness scares me sometimes!' Reb said in exasperation.

'I am only giving you an analysis of the facts, Reb, I am not as squeamish as you Minerans.'

'Ok, you two, knock it off,' the sergeant said. He had known Reb and the doctor long enough to speak out of rank. The captain wandered over to the body and draped a sheet over it. 'Doc, please show some respect, these poor souls have been plucked from their lives and unwillingly been experimented on and used as weapons. They are as much a victim as we are.'

'Can you imagine how formidable they would be if you put armour on these guys?' Reb enquired.

'They will be a challenging opponent, Reb, but you just change tactics. We favour kinetic weapons out of tradition, but they are mere flesh and bone. We have various weapons that can liquefy them inside of their armour.'

'There is something else,' the doctor said, using one long arm to pick up a tray hidden behind the body. On it was the arrow that he had removed from Sam. A white cloth obscured the rest of the contents.

'You recognise this, of course. You all saw the feed showing Sam being skewered to the steel block with it.'

'Yes, we are aware of the implications of someone using an ancestral weapon, Doctor. Reb reported that it was some form of ceramic model designed to pass through the Dia Kuklos.'

'That's partially correct. The inner workings are a little more complicated and use composites of natural materials. As you know, someone, who is as yet unknown, took over the Dia Kuklos and shot Sam from the rear. What you are unaware of is that Reb, wasting my cleansing fluid to create a wall of fire, didn't hold back the enemy for a second. These did.' The doc removed the white cloth with a flourish to show another nine arrows. 'These ancestral arrows of yours are a nightmare to extract, and I challenge you to clean and reset one. I had to put the heads in with some Gnarva ants to remove all the organic matter. They are really clever you know, using an excreted acid from their abdomens to break down the bone into a digestible jelly.' He saw the sergeant try to suppress a shudder and smiled. 'Interesting', he thought, 'he's squeamish about insects, what does he feel about me'?

'Sorry, Doc, you have lost us. Are you saying the person who shot Sam also shot at,' gesturing with his hand at the covered body on the table the captain questioned, 'their own soldiers?'

'I cannot say who shot at who, Captain. All I know is that I extracted eight of these from the heads of eight soldiers. This is what caused the front line of their advance to falter and not the wall of fire.'

'There are ten on the tray, Doc, including Sam's. Where did the extra one come from?' Reb enquired.

'A keen eye as always, Reb, and I am glad you asked,'

he replied with an iniquitous grin. 'Please bear in mind the unknown shooter had less than a minute to fire these before we regained control or they relinquished control of the Dia Kuklos. Judging by the angle that it was protruding from the body of a soldier, he was shot in the leg while on the floor to prevent the shaft from opening up. He had previously been slain by a bullet to the head. This anomaly was out of context with the precision shooting that I had catalogued so far. Each of the other eight had gone through an eye socket. Upon further inspection I found this scratched into the surface. I am assuming that it is a message, albeit cryptic. I have sent scans of the shaft to cryptology an hour ago. Alas, so far to no avail.' He held out the shaft for inspection. 'Please be careful how you handle it, it is primed and ready to spring open.'

Reb took the shaft, holding it firmly at the front end. Holding out of the shadows that the three of them made while trying to see the text he saw §15412. 'I've seen this section symbol recently.' He walked to the doctor's wall terminal, gestured with his hand to activate it and requested, 'Show the markings found on the surveillance cameras that were taken from Sam Shepard's room.'

A large portion of the wall illuminated showing the archived pictures of the tiny surveillance cameras that were used to monitor Sam.

'It's not definitive but that scratched § looks awfully like Sam's handwriting,' the captain said with trepidation in his voice. 'You know this makes no sense, as if things weren't confusing enough.' The captain sat on the edge of the table, oblivious or uncaring that he was next to the cadaver. The strain of the last few days showed on his already lined face.

'When will he be available to talk, Doc?' Reb asked as

he passed the arrow back. The doctor held out the tray for Reb to place it back carefully.

'Before we move on to Sam, I would like to obscure the picture further by adding that the sequence on the other side of the Dia Kuklos could not have happened within the fifty-three seconds that we lost control of it. I replicated the historic weapon used to fire these,' he said, waving around an arrow as if it were an innocuous toothpick. 'I modified it to increase the rate of fire and timed how long it would take to fire off nine shots and carve the message. Then you have to consider the pause between the initial shot and those that took down your assailants,' he said, looking at Reb. 'I speculate that the assassin was disturbed while shooting at Sam. The weapon has proven to be accurate and therefore there was no reason to miss. Further analysis indicates the only possible explanation is there must be a time dilatation on our side from their perspective.'

'Wouldn't multiple weapons solve this?'

'The forensics on the shaft show identical micro abrasions indicating they were all fired from the same weapon.'

'You've given us much to consider, Doc, thank you.'

'As for Sam, I have concentrated the initial regeneration process on his respiratory system as I had to transfuse oxygenated cells into his blood to keep him alive. We have just finished rebuilding his face, and we found another underlying problem which I had to correct, but nothing serious. His body will be numb and immobile for another day as I have not finished with his leg and shoulder. I suppose I could wake him if you can give me some preparation time.'

'I'll give you half an hour to prepare him, Doc; we need answers,' the captain said as he walked to the closed door. With a gentle swipe of his hand, it opened with a fluidic grace by sliding silently into the wall. 'Oh, Doc, I appreciate the effort to mask the corpse's odour. Being soldiers it's nothing we haven't smelt before, but dear God, what is that smell?'

The doc was clearly taken aback. 'Oh, I thought you would like it. Lieutenant Kallistrate always smells of the small yellow flower from her hometown, to mask her odour, I forget its name. I used the essence of the Capranulnka plant. It grows in the swamps near my brood's dwelling. We use it in our wedding ceremonies, it also has excellent medicinal properties.'

'You actually like this, Doc? I'd laugh, but it would mean I have to take in huge lung-fulls of this dreadful aroma.' Reb reached up to put his hand on the doc's shoulder. 'Wake him up, Doc, we'll see you in the infirmary in a bit.'

The captain did a turn around to face the doctor. 'Was there any temporal degradation?'

'If you mean temporal displacement degeneration, no. They are from Earth at this point in time. I will have the results from the lab on trace particulates from the clothing, skin and lungs soon. Hopefully, we can narrow down the region that they came from via pollen, pollution et al.'

'Erm. That's something I suppose. Oh, Doc, I suggest that you don't ever tell Lieutenant Kallistrate that she smells.' Doing a second about-face, he walked off.

CHAPTER 14

The trio stood alongside Sam's bed. The hair on his head had been shaved off, and the new facial tissue still had a baby-pink look. It would be sensitive for a while, Reb reflected. He had been on the receiving end of Doc's ministrations on a few occasions. The body was born with the genetic instructions to grow itself from a simple cell. It was surprisingly easy to convince it to rebuild itself. Convincing it to do so at speed was the hard and painful part.

On the whole, the doctor had done, as he always did, a good job. For some reason hair follicles never grew back. If Sam wanted, he could have whiskers implanted into the new tissue later, allowing him to grow a beard across the whole of his face. Reb had had his whiskers removed decades ago. Not that he got much chance to grow a beard anyway, but that was another matter. 'One which Sam would stumble across', he thought with a smile.

Sam's leg was out of the bed sheet, and the regeneration unit was encouraging the body to build up the new bones and muscle. Doc would have localised pain relief affecting the area; otherwise, Sam would be awake and screaming. The act of re-growing a nerve end at such a rapid rate was more painful than the event that caused the wound in the first place. A smaller unit was working on his shoulder, with a prong inserted into the wound. It would withdraw over the course of about eight hours, rebuilding the shoulder from the inside out as it went.

'How long until he is on his feet, Doc?' Reb enquired.

'Two days as his body mass is much lower than yours, so it's easier to repair. I am assuming this is due to Earth having a lower gravity.'

'I noticed in the file that you lowered the gravity in any room that Sam entered so I followed your lead. The gravity in the infirmary will remain at Earth's norm for a day or so. He will notice considerable discomfort elsewhere on the station. Do I have your permission to increase his muscle mass and strengthen his bones, Captain?'

'Do what you can for him in the time frame you have specified, Doc. I need him on his feet and walking unaided. Oh, Doc, it might be advisable for you to stand back as he regains consciousness.'

'Caution noted, Captain,' he said, with a nod of his head. He opened a valve on the IV line to allow the anti-sedative through. When Sam had first come through the Dia Kuklos, the doctor had never seen a real human before. He knew nothing of their chemistry, physiology or tolerances and the central database was of little help. It wasn't until later that the information had come through from Minera. He secretly feared that he might have turned Sam into a cabbage. He stepped back from the bed after the small vial had emptied into the line and out of consideration for Sam dimmed the lights further. 'You should have about five minutes with him before he'll fall under again, but please give him a few seconds, Captain, he will be disoriented at first.' He withdrew into the shadows.

'Thank you, Doc.'

It took Sam a full minute and a half to open his eyes and only after Reb's impatient prompting. Reb had seen movement under the eyelids and recognised that Sam was listening for clues as to his whereabouts without giving away his conscious state. The four occupants had remained silent, waiting for Sam to wake up. All he would be sensing is the noise and movement from medical devices on him, around the room and the faint hum and vibration of the station itself as well as the rustle of clothing nearby.

'Open your eyes, Sam, you're in the infirmary.' He said, 'I know you're awake.'

'Reb, is that you? I thought we'd both bought the farm,' Sam said through his rebuilt mouth. He opened and closed his jaw as if it was stiff or wanted to click. 'You stitched my tongue back in. Doesn't hurt as much as I thought it would.' His lids were only fractionally open. The dimmed lights seeming bright to his unaccustomed eyes. 'I can't move.'

Reb could see the strain of him trying to move his body in his neck and face. 'Calm down Sam, you're going to be fine. The doctor has immobilised you while he heals the rest of your body. You will be glad to know that he has fully repaired your face, although I am sorry, but there was nothing he could do about your God-awful looks.' He saw Sam smile. Humour in the face of adversity, helps every time.

'I don't understand, how long have I been unconscious?'

'Less than two days, Sam,' said the doctor. He was keeping out of sight, allowing Sam's body to block his view. 'I am your doctor. We haven't been formally introduced. Your physiology is quite interesting; I might write a paper on it. I don't understand why you pompously called yourselves Homo sapiens though, Homo morionis would be more apt. I digress. I have repaired your respiratory system, mouth and face, and we are still working on your non-life-threatening injuries of shoulder and leg. It might interest you to note that you had a large aortic aneurysm forming. If left undetected you would have had less than six months left. A silver lining to all this discomfort.'

Sam tried to look at Reb, the restricted movement in his neck making it awkward. 'What happened?'

'Thirty assailants made their way through the enclave. They must have had help.' Reb's voice sounded melancholic. 'There are two entrances to the distorted space we call the Mineran Enclave. The one through the warehouse and a small path in the hills. The small guard post there had been neutralised with a sleep gas and the gates opened. Interestingly the traitor wasn't willing to kill his own kind, but he or she did give away the location of a secret installation and aided interlopers. The computer had been programmed to see the intruders as sheep, and the outpost had enough vehicles to carry thirty people exactly.' Reb looked into Sam's eyes. 'Sam, the only thing they did was to come after you. They weren't after the Dia Kuklos. In fact, they seemed ignorant of its workings.' He let those words sink in for a second.

'Do you remember we temporarily lost control of the Dia Kuklos?'

Sam nodded, his eye looking towards the contraption on his chest. 'When I got pinned to the cube.'

'Yes, we have reason to believe the two attacks were separate. Sam, does Section Symbol and 15412 mean anything to you?'

'I don't understand.'

The sergeant handed a display tablet to Reb, who held it for Sam to see. 'Sam, someone shot you, and then they targeted the attackers before leaving this message.' Reb saw recognition flare up in Sam's eyes. 'What is it, Sam?'

'It's a date, an important one, a small victory in a large pointless conflict. We were on patrol in the hills of a friendly province. We stumbled across an insurgent ambush which was about to ensnare an unsuspecting UN convoy. Near the top ridge, there was a group with portable guided missile launchers, and a few had brand new Russian Dragunov sniper rifles. Below us in the valley, there were over fifty rebels holed up. We timed it right and silently took out the snipers and other soldiers with the launchers. Using their own ordnance and the advantage of elevated height we broke the ambush below before they could spring the trap. I personally took out twenty with the Dragunov.' Sleep was slurring Sam's speech now as he struggled to remain awake. 'It turned out to be two factions. One was using the other as cannon fodder. We saved a lot of UN soldiers that day.'

'I read the report from your file, Sam. It was all very commendable, but what does the message mean?' the captain asked impatiently. 'It looks like your handwriting; why would you have sent it?'

Confusion crossed Sam's face, followed quickly by fatigue. 'I didn't send it, I got shot.'

'If you did send it, Sam, what would it mean?' Reb asked diplomatically. Sam's eyes were closing with weariness.

'I suppose it would mean that I saved you from an

ambush and took them out with their own weapons.' Sam's eyes looked weary now, and his face was starting to look gaunt. The conversation having taken more out of him than he really had to give.

'That's it for today, gentlemen, my patient needs to rest.' The doctor ushered them to the door. Sam was asleep before the doctor had finished speaking.

~*~

Nearly forty-eight hours later Sam awoke for the second time. He still felt tired, and his mind was as woolly as an angora rabbit. He managed to sit up in his bed, noting the room he was in was a typically bland and utilitarian hospital room. He was glad to see that the apparatus had been removed from his chest and he slowly moved various parts of his body as to reassure himself they were still there and still working. Rubbing his chin with his hand, he noticed patches of stubble.

The doctor had observed Sam's movements from the next room. The adjoining observation window was set to opaque on the patient's side to prevent any movement or light from interfering with Sam's recovery. He put the samples that he was working on back into the fridge and walked into Sam's room.

The reception he received was unexpected, but later on, with reflection and hindsight, it was understandable. The doctor realised that Sam, having got his feet on the floor, would have noticed even in his convalescing capacity, that his body was more toned and muscular. The doctor had not reset the gravity in the infirmary, and the moderately small tweaks he had made to Sam's would make him roughly 50 per cent stronger and heavier than before. With exercise, he could double his initial strength potential. He wouldn't be a superhuman, but he would be able to cope with the normal gravity of the station and outfight most of his own kind.

The doctor saw Sam turn towards him, shock and fear showing in his face. The doctor caught the portable regeneration unit as it was thrown towards him. It wouldn't have done any damage, but they were expensive and hard to obtain. He admired Sam's courage and audacity, as he attacked bare-handed. The doctor was mainly concerned with Sam's safety and so squirted him in the face from his nostrils with the foul smelling liquid that came directly from the stomach and incapacitated most opponents in seconds. Pre-civilisation, it was a means of capturing their prey alive, but for the last millennia or so it was easier to farm for food. He had always enjoyed the annual games on his planet. Entrants would come from all over the galaxy to compete. Twenty combatants against one naked Preialeiac, gladiatorial style. True, he was not allowed to kill and eat them nor could they try and kill him which reduced the thrill a little. Each opposing warrior had their personal choice of stun weapons, all he had was what nature had endowed him with. He still had his mesothorax appendages then. Happy, glorious memories. He had decided that temporarily shedding his mid-section arms would help him to become more visually acceptable to bipeds.

He caught Sam before he collapsed and placed him on the bed and the put the apparatus back on the cabinet by the bed. Taking a cloth, he cleaned Sam's face. 'Bravo, Sam,' he gently whispered. 'Many have cowered in the same situation.'

Leaving Sam with the duty nurse, he arranged for Reb to be present upon Sam's reawakening.

'Welcome back.' Reb passed him a glass of green

liquid. 'It'll take the taste away,' he explained.

'Thanks.' He took a sip then swilled his mouth full before swallowing.

'I have trained with the Preialeiac, that's the doctor's species, and have been squirted on a few occasions.' Upon seeing Sam's reaction, 'Yeah, that was the doctor.'

'The doctor?'

'Don't worry about it, I would have introduced you two after the tunnels. He was coming to meet us.' He shrugged and raised his arms as if to say "shit happens". 'The doc's not offended, I think he was slightly impressed by you, to tell the truth.'

'What was that he sprayed me with?'

'Er, grossly the fluid is from one of his stomachs. Just be grateful it wasn't gastric acid. He said to say that it's not too dissimilar to the Artic Petrel on your planet. He's been like a child with a new toy since being given access to the Earth database. Having previously written several papers on similar life forms' variations in differing ecosystems, I think he has found the topic of his next academic work.'

A disembodied voice echoed around the room. 'Is it safe to come in now?'

Looking at Sam, 'Shall we try again?'

Sam nodded as a head appeared at the top of the door frame. The doctor was peering in cautiously. Sam could not help but stare. The head was insectoid with a chitin look and with vicious-looking mandibles next to a large toothed mouth. The only comparable human features that he could see was that the doctor had two front-facing eyes, two semi-vertical slits for nostrils and a ginormous mouth.

'I do apologise for scaring you earlier Sam, that was not my intention.' The disembodied head said with a flash

144

of razor-sharp looking teeth. 'Evolution designed my species to be predators and as such our visage instils fear upon our prey and alas, sometimes our allies also.' The doctor stepped around the frame, filling the full height of the doorway. He was dressed in a full-length dark blue doctor's coat that was buttoned up, his bare chitin legs protruding from the bottom. He looked down at himself. 'I took the liberty of copying earth doctor's attire, although I found it strange how your physicians and butchers wear the same garment. I chose to colour it blue to avoid any confusion.'

He walked slowly across and held out a long arm which ended in an armoured crustaceous like hand. Sam shook it.

'They just call me the Doctor or Doc, as my name is unpronounceable with your limited vocal range. I am happy to make your acquaintance,' he said, shaking Sam's hand.

From Sam's point of view, it was similar to having a very strong crab in his hand. Instead of legs wrapping around his palm, it had eight powerful fingers. Sam had to crane his neck to look up to the doctor, although being sat up in bed didn't really help.

'I'm sorry I attacked you Doc, I wasn't sure wha... I mean who you were and with everyone trying to kill me in the last few days...'

'Most understandable, think nothing of it.'

'Right, now the introductions are over, I have to get on with the investigation. We have a few tenuous leads to chase.' Reb placed a large carton on the bed with the words "Bioform Environmental Exoskeleton – BEE". 'Before you release him, Doc, please can you get him into this and show him how to put it on and take it off correctly,' smiling as he said so.

The doctor bowed in acquiescence.

Reb looked at Sam 'I need you to do as Doc asks, without question, Sam. I wanted to be here when we gave you some of the background information and answered your questions. Alas, that's impossible now as I have to head back to Minera to help with the investigation. The doctor will fill you in. In fact, being the oldest on the station he's the most qualified to tell you about Earth history. I know it's a lot to ask, but please trust us, we are trying to help.' Without waiting for a reply, he put his hand on Sam's shoulder and left.

Sam looked up at the doctor once again, feeling vulnerable in the face of such a tall non-human. He took a moment to examine his leg and shoulder. Besides being baby-pink and hairless where the new skin had been grown, it looked healthy. He felt around his face and pushed a finger into his mouth to check his teeth. 'You grew new teeth?'

'You grew new teeth, Sam, I just encouraged your body to do so. It's not a technology that is widely available as it is prohibitively expensive,' indicating the small regeneration unit next to the bed, 'The unit you threw at me costs more than the net worth of your planet.' He opened a seamless wall panel with a light touch of his finger, the door appearing and unlatching silently. Retrieving a small hand mirror he gave it to Sam.

'If you require I can implant new hair follicles for your facial hair, the regeneration process omits to grow hair. It is not possible to implant them in the first week as we have to wait until the tissue stabilises.' Noticing Sam slide a hand over the top of his now bald head he continued. 'That hair will grow back normally, I had to shave it and part of your chest hair for medical hygiene reasons, I'm afraid.'

'So what's next then, Doc?' Sam asked while looking at his new, and at the same time, old unchanged face.

'I can release you for duty in two or three days. I need to run some more tests, and you need to exercise to generate new muscle and acclimatise to your stronger anatomy.'

'Stronger?'

'I took the liberty of slightly instigating an increase in your muscle and bone density. It should be complete within twenty-four hours. You will need to exercise rigorously for twelve hours to aid the process. Your strength to muscle ratio will increase by a factor of 100 per cent. The increase in density gives you strength without the extra bulk. You will be a lot stronger and heavier than you look. Consider the monkeys on your planet, you have approximately 95 per cent the same DNA and yet they are three times stronger than humans because of their muscle density. Without this modification, you would have struggled with the gravity outside of this room.

Sam moved the bed sheet from his lower torso, he hadn't been this buff since the height of his army career. 'You experimented on me?' he said in exasperation.

'Technically true as I have never seen or operated on a human before, but no, it is a simple procedure if you have a regenerator and understand genetics as I do. I did ask Captain Sophus before commencing. I am sorry if I have offended you, I thought you would be grateful.'

'Sorry, Doc, I'm having trouble processing everything. I didn't mean to snap. If you're so advanced with your medicine, why haven't you cured Emliton of his narcolepsy?' Sam enquired.

'Emliton is one of the bravest bipeds I have ever fought alongside. The number of lives he has saved is immeasurable. However, such encounters take a toll on ones such as he, for as fierce and heroic as he was, he was twice as kind and gentle. The visage of each life that could not be saved remains with him, haunting him until one day he simply stopped. He sleeps to turn off, to forget, but the day-mares are the same as his nightmares. He finds no rest, and he asks for no forgiveness for his failings. In truth, there is nothing to forgive, but he will not forgive himself for not being,' Doc paused while reflecting, 'for not being godlike. That would have been the only way to save the ones we lost. I fought alongside him in twenty-seven campaigns. Not once did he falter in our endeavours and never did his resolve waver. He mentally broke on a planet where the inhabitants resembled bipedal babies. Whole armies of tiny, infant-like soldiers littered the battlefields, small, tiny things crushed into the dirt. He fought savagely for weeks. In the urban combat he killed more Inchethslar with his blade than he did with his rifle, shielding himself with one dead body to the next intended Inchethslar. He was glorious, he should have been born a Preialeiac, and I would be proud to call him my brood brother.'

'Why are police involved in wars? I don't understand.'

'They call themselves police, Sam, but they are military through and through. They are assigned to aid the regular planet side police, to provide a brutal and swift reinforcement where necessary. Every planet has specialised, highly trained crack troops and the best of them wish to join us for we get the special jobs. The ones on the frontline where a delicate touch is needed by an iron claw, sorry, I mean hand. The Minerans alone guard the Dia Kuklos, and so this causes a mysterious enigma as all of their bases are secret and hidden.' The doctor turned from his instruments to look at Sam. 'The populace feared a heavily armed police force and the backlash from them when the army was called in for an emergency caused more harm than the original problem. So it was deemed necessary to have a special force that straddled the two. One that polices the army and the police which can also be called in for civil emergencies. It was made up of the highest calibre recruits, ones with proven track records of honour and integrity. They were to stay honed by fighting on the front lines as specialists, where their honour could be maintained and become public record. These were men and women to be loved by all, bar criminals, for these would see no mercy if they resisted.' Returning to the original topic, he continued, 'Emliton will cure himself when he is ready. There is counselling if he requires it. We Preialeiac do not suffer so, we live, we die, we go to the divine place and eventually we are reborn and the wheel continues to turn. The doctor produced horrendous sounds that physically hurt Sam's ears and he could feel the inaudible frequencies vibrating through his body. 'As said, fear not death, as both life and death are transient phases of a greater cycle of existence.' Seeing confusion on Sam's face he placed a hand on Sam's shoulder accompanied with a sound that was similar to a crab running across a glass floor. 'We are a very old, and some say ferocious race, we have had time to reflect on the deeper meaning of existence.'

Tossing Sam a brown coverall from the box on the bed he said, 'If you can strip and put this on, I will try to explain how it works.'

Sam caught the garment with one muscled arm. He was surprised that it was heavier than it appeared and that it had an odd leathery feel to it, but the flexibility of silk.

'This is the BEE suit. You will wear this as your

standard garment while on duty. It is your reactive body armour and environmental suit. You saw it partially absorb and spread the pressure of impact from projectile weapons upon Reb's body. Once you are strong enough, the physical impact will have little effect. It has a greater effect on energy weapons and can act with the aid of the pull over the headpiece as a full bio suit. It can filter out toxins and pass on oxygen for short periods. Sam, this is an organic suit, its absorption is actually the suit digesting the energy. It can only consume a finite amount. Do not make the fatal assumption that you are invulnerable.'

Sam paused. 'I'm wearing a digestive system? You want me to wear this?'

'It is a non-sentient life form; it has not got any organs per se. It consumes mainly energy, not people. Think of it as a protective suit of moss or lichen that consumes the energy from daylight, only in this case it can happily feed on a military laser for its tea.'

Sam couldn't see any fastening on the front and so pressed the edges together. They gradually bonded, merging, leaving no visible trace of a seam.

'With each suit, you get a controller. Reb calls his Bob. Bob is safely tucked away somewhere in the Universe and is Reb's direct contact to the ISPAW. Without the suit, he has no way of contacting Bob. No one else can wear a suit after it has bonded with the designated body, hence the channel is secure. Are you with me so far?'

'Ok.'

'Bob controls the suit. I do not know how, so don't ask. Your suit will help you gain muscle mass over the next 24 hours as it will add resistance to your movements, making it harder to move. On low gravity worlds it will, when required, add resistance to prevent you from appearing overly strong. It can operate the other way when you require added strength. It can enhance your strength and carrying capabilities.'

He gently ushered Sam into the next room where a large ring floated in the centre. 'Your first exercise, Sam. Jump up; you might not have noticed but the baby-grow kind of sock booties have now formed into firm boots. Be assured these will never give you blisters and the suit will regulate your temperature so you should never sweat.' Watching Sam jump up, he instructed him to insert his boots into the foot sockets, grab the hand rails and scrunch. 'Shrink the diameter of the ring, it and the suit will fight you, then you have to push it out again. Use your stomach muscles, not just your arms and legs.'

Sam tried to curl into a ball, pulling the ring with him. It did contract, leaving no visible trace of warping or any mechanical means of interlacing. He pushed back out, feeling the muscles around his body tense.

'The ring will vary the effort required and change aspect and direction, making you use different muscles as you progress. The suit will add an accumulative amount of resistance as you acclimatise. The ring will slowly lose its circular shape as your arms and legs point in various directions.' Sam continued to scrunch and unravel as the doctor continued to talk.

'What has Reb told you about the Dia Kuklos and how they were formed?'

'Not much, only that a catastrophic occurrence caused them.'

'Well, that's certainly an understatement. There are approximately 300 known to exist, primarily they are clustered in close proximity. Usually they have been formed due to great battles using forces of such magnitude as to distort the fabric of space. Has Reb mentioned the Overseer?' Upon seeing Sam's nod, he proceeded. 'Three-quarters of those occurred prior to the Overseer's appearance, their creation lost in the annals of time. More than likely because there were no victors. All bar fourteen occurred during the great wars that brought forth the wrath of the Overseer.'

Struggling for breath as the ring went through a phase of extreme muscle burning contractions, Sam said, 'Fourteen. Is it a coincidence that Earth has fourteen Dia Kuklos?'

'No. Earth has been through two major climate changing apocalyptic populace extinctive wars in the past. You are not the original inhabitants, Sam. You are a very distant relative.'

'Ok,' he said, sceptically looking at the doctor. 'So what happened? Who were we/ they at war with?'

'Ah, this, I think, is the part Reb would have liked to have been here to explain. I do carry the race memory of our part in this unfortunate occurrence, albeit small.' Noticing Sam had stopped, he gestured for him to continue.

'Firstly, you have to understand that your planet is much older than your scientists believe. At least twice as old. Eight million years ago the race of beings that populated your planet were a barbaric, fearsome race. For me to say this, it should give you an indication of how bad they really were. No one could figure out how they suddenly became a spacefaring race in such a short period of time. They made giant leaps in technology that they clearly didn't comprehend. The destruction they caused to their, your, planet was catastrophic in itself. They poured from system to system in ships that beggared belief. They were so badly constructed that no one knew how the crews could survive in them. They waged war after war, decimating systems. Not for the profits or accumulation of land, but just barbaric slaughter. Documents recovered from destroyed ships showed studies of various and escalating genocide techniques. The scale of the weapons used became larger and larger until one day they actually destroyed a heavily populated planet. The ISPAW were slow to act, thinking the Overseer would step in. When he spoke, his message was clear, work together to resolve this. We had to police within the spheres borders ourselves. He would only intervene if ISPAW members went to war with each other, or as our sphere of influence expanded outwards across the universe, we faced an external opponent whose technology was beyond ours and would cause catastrophic loss of life. Two member systems of ISPAW made the incorrect assumption that this meant the Overseer had become impotent over the millennia and took advantage to seize neighbouring planets and systems. They were dealt with swiftly, and they did not have clean deaths. It was as if their planets were nudged, their orbits quickly decayed around their suns, and they burnt up. All military or parliamentary craft and installations that were off-world were also destroyed. The few thousand inhabitants that lived elsewhere were doomed to roam the universe never having a true home. They are still a living reminder of angering the Overseer. Sorry, I digress, history is a passion of mine – my species lives so long that we remember a lot of it personally. The ISPAW went to war. Over the course of weeks, your ancestors were driven back to their home planet. There they fought valiantly in a war they could not win. With their last dying breath, they overloaded the fourteen prototype singularity drives that they had secretly been working on, hoping to take the planet and ISPAW fleet with them. Your planet was decimated, the explosions went inward, distorting the fabric of space and killing 99 per cent of life on your planet. The ISPAW withdrew, and the planet was deemed uninhabitable.'

Sam was silent now, still working away, not quite knowing what to make of Earth's history.

'Three billion years later another race sprang up. History repeated itself, a hoard of technologically advanced savages swept across the universe with no discernible pattern. They swooped into systems like pirates, randomly, and caused incalculable damage and loss of life. One of their ships was disabled in a brief fight and the crew taken alive. Like their predecessors, they could create and make use of technological advances but without fully understanding it. It was, at first, assumed that an outside influence was orchestrating them for nefarious gain. We were half right, evolution on your planet had twice designed a brain system that worked on a frequency so close to our long distance communication systems that over time, unconsciously, they learnt everything. Their only downfall was the fact that they were an immature race with little or no concept of strategy that allowed us to prevail; they were that strong. Eventually, they too were pushed back to their home planet. They had developed shields of such magnitude that our orbital bombardments were futile. The ISPAW could see they were designing and creating newer hybrid ships with the mixed technologies from many of the races. A drastic plan was formulated, one which we hope never to re-enact. The larger of your two moons was destroyed, the resulting gravitation forces pulled your planet's crust apart, the shields died in the chaos of earthquakes and an orbit bombardment commenced. Your planet was left a glowing cinder so as not to allow this to happen again.'

The doctor steadied the ring and offered a chitin hand to assist Sam to climb down. 'Stretch and cool down exercise, ten minutes to rehydrate and then we hit the viscous pool.'

'Then we appeared,' Sam said, rather subdued. The initial anger had dissipated.

'Yes, it was a conundrum, 3.5 million years ago the ISPAW could see single cell life forming on your planet and they were not up to commit planet-wide genocide again, even on amoebas. A series of satellites were set up to enclose your solar system and block out the communication frequencies. It was hoped that you would evolve normally.'

'Where do the Minerans come into this? Reb said they had been here from the beginning.'

'Well, for your beginning they were. Shortly after the first war, the Universe Police formed at the Overseer's behest. In between that and the first amoeba forming on your planet, the Minerans had a little run-in with the Overseer. Eventually, they were enlisted and sent to police Dia Kuklos around the universe. They're actually a specialised subset of the universe police, it's a multispecies agency. The Minerans' history is a highly guarded secret, as much as the Dia Kuklos themselves. They are, as a race, ashamed of their ancestral history. That's why they were so upset seeing the Spica Sagitta in your back.'

Sam continued to exercise that day, with the doctor providing him with fluids that were so nourishing he never realised that he didn't actually eat anything. After the viscous pool, there were gravity-enhanced endurance exercises, which were then followed by so many other tortuous regimes.

CHAPTER 15

Collapsing on the hospital bed, Sam lay there exhausted. He had given it everything he had, and whatever the doctor had been giving him in the drinks was a body builder's dream elixir. Sam dreaded to think what he was like under the BEE suit. He could only imagine that he was rank with sweat, thankfully it sealed in the stench.

'Well done, Sam, a marvellous effort. We need to get you out of the BEE, freshened up and massaged to loosen up those newly developed muscles.'

Sam looked at the doctor's hands. 'Massage?' he enquired.

Clicking the harsh-looking fingers together the doctor replied, 'We have a physiotherapist here on the station, Sam. I find the staff here prefer him for some reason.' A wicked, tooth-riddled grin spread across his face.

Sam tried to pry apart the suit. He found it difficult to even dig his fingers beneath the collar. Try as he might, the invisible seam would not open.

'There's a sensor in the arm which informs your partner you wish to communicate. He or she has been listening in of course, but etiquette requires you to inform him or her that you want to correspond. It's not necessary to put your finger in your ear, but you have to at least press firmly just in front. The vibrations are sent up your arm and through your finger to produce sound as it hits your eardrum – a silent means of conversing. The suit can manage it without your finger if an important message needs to be conveyed, Reb says, and I quote, 'It's a bloody horrible feeling'.

Sam inserted his right index finger into his ear. 'Er, hello.'

'Hello, Sam,' a gender-neutral voice replied.

He looked futilely at the doctor for guidance. A rotating hand movement either meant carry on or he was indicating that he wanted to eviscerate Sam's organs with his sharp, crab-like talons.

'Hi, how do I remove the suit?'

'We don't recommend you remove the BEE suit, Sam. This would leave you vulnerable. Without your body armour you are at an increased risk of sustaining damage.'

'I think I'm safe enough for now; please can you tell me how to remove the suit?' At that the BEE suit peeled from Sam's chest in two halves. Glad to be free, he rapidly removed his arms. God, he looked pumped. Not the full-on bodybuilder look, but definitely buff. He couldn't make out what was missing for a second, then he looked at his chest. Only half had been shaved by the doctor but now it was as smooth as a baby's bottom. 'What the –' he exclaimed, quickly removing the lower part of the garment, displaying a smooth, hairless torso and limbs. He looked in alarm at the doctor and back at himself. 'It ate my hair! It's eaten my fucking hair! What? Why?'

'Apate moaned about that too the first time; she still

refuses to wear the hood even after all these years. She now admits that she rather enjoys the extra smooth, silky feel of her skin now. She says it gives her a nice glow. Unlike you, she only gets to wear hers on away missions when she's acting as backup for Reb.' Seeing this was not dissipating Sam's annoyance, 'The suit has to be in direct contact with the skin in order for it to protect you, Sam. It simply absorbs the hairs and top epidermal layer. It's not eating you.'

~*~

After a few days of tweaking the medication and rigorous exercise, the doctor examined the results from the last medical scan of Sam. He could not believe that one life form could have housed so many parasitic diseases, viruses, bacteria and deadly pathogens. Before he could start Sam's reconstruction and rehabilitation, he'd have to purge him of these potentially harmful threats. If ever the doctor needed a test subject for incubation, he knew where to look in the future. These humans, as they called themselves, bred like vermin and were as filthy as. The strangest thing was that having spent time with Sam, he'd grown to actually like him. He'd kept samples of Sam's infected blood, knowing that when Sam returned to Earth on active duty he would have to be re-infected. The whole idea of having a human on the team was to have someone who could investigate on the ground and blend in because he was a native. Most off-world antagonists would class him as a clueless native, although their automated scans might pick up on the anomalous fact that his blood and tissue were medically pristine. The doctor made a mental note that he should also perform a similar cleansing process to remove any off-world germs or antibodies from Sam as well as replace the earthbound ones back. He found it strange that this lateral thinking was not natural to him. The process of thinking out of the box was rubbing off from Sam. He could see why Erebus liked humans. They were inquisitive, imaginative and often random in their actions. These features were surprisingly rare amongst the other races.

'I can clear you for duty Sam – but if you agree to sign up? I must warn you that you will most likely spend a minimum of a year away for training and it will be far more rigorous than what we have done in the last few days. You will also have to become familiar with the standard, and to some extent, the non-standard equipment used throughout the Universe. You will be required to learn the characteristics of each race and their technology. Apparently one of your redeeming factors was the solitary and nomadic life you have lived for the past few years. You will not really be missed while you are away training.'

'A year's not too bad, it sounds like there is a lot to see.'

'Ah, that's an ISPAW year.' The doctor quickly used a tablet computer he withdrew from his pocket. 'It equates to approximately 3.8 Earth years.' Seeing the puzzled look on Sam's face he continued. 'Most planets base their chronological system on the daily rotation of their planet and their annual orbit around their sun. In a multi-system society such as ours, that becomes problematic. The ISPAW calculated the average year by using a 10 per cent trimmed average of known planets inhabited by intelligent life forms within the original ISPAW sphere. This became the ISPAW Standard Year.'

Sam later learned that the ISPAW defines a year as 327

x 37 hour days, with 100 seconds per minute and 100 minutes per hour or 120,990,000 seconds per year. Any time reference in documents had to contain a local planet time reference and the ISPAW equivalent. The Minerans had been instructed to introduce the concept of standardised seconds, minutes and hours to Earth a long time ago. Due to the Earth's rotation and small orbit of the sun, they only managed to encourage the adoption of a standard second, which humans later defined as the amount of time a cesium-133 atom to perform 9,192,631,770 complete oscillations.

~*~

Reb and Captain Sophus arrived shortly after the doctor had removed Sam's breakfast tray.

'Is he fit for duty, Doc?' The captain enquired. 'We have a development in the investigation that we think Sam should be part of.'

'Sam has made an excellent recovery; his strength is up threefold in truth. He hasn't even noticed that the gravity is at Mineran norm.' He looked at Sam with a shark-like smile. 'Although I must report that I have recently become aware that by my standards he's practically blind.' Everyone turned to Sam and then back to the doctor for clarification. 'He has an even more limited view of the light spectrum than you do, Captain, and I consider you to be a partially blind species.'

He walked across to Sam and gently laid his crustaceous hand on Sam's head. 'Sam, please describe the room.'

Looking somewhat confused, he replied, 'It's a typical hospital room, a little drab and colourless, but no different from a hundred others I've been in.'

'Sam, the walls and cupboard doors are covered in your medical readouts and charts.' Pointing to the door behind Sam, 'that one is showing the oxygen ratio and performance of your lungs in real time.'

Sam's head swivelled around, he looked at several cupboards hoping to see something.

'It appears, Captain, that humans can only see from red to violet. I suspected something was wrong when Sam repeatedly ignored the exercise equipment's instructions. As you know, most of your data projections and information technology utilises the ultraviolet frequency.'

Looking again at Sam, Reb requested, 'Describe the triptych that you saw on Urser's arm.'

'It was scar tissue, almost making the shape of a triangle.'

'There's a colour code on the segments to indicate the severity of the crime,' he commented. 'The 3D hologram in the communications room, you didn't see the biological readouts overlaid for each person or chemical analysis on pertinent items?' It was more of a statement than a question.

'No,' he said with uncertainty in his voice. 'It was just a 3D video.'

'He can't be left on his own on the station. He'll bloody well walk right out of an air lock,' the captain said in amazement. 'Doc, we don't have time to sort this out now, if you can rectify this it'll have to wait.' Looking at Sam, 'get suited up, Sam, there's a meeting in fifteen minutes and then we are off.' Nodding at Reb and the doctor, he walked out.

'As I have discharged you, Sam, I will excuse myself. I need to prepare for the meeting.' The doctor walked into the other room, his head barely clearing the extra tall

161

doorway.

Feeling oddly exposed undressing in front of Reb he turned around. 'Ok, I understand what they meant about me not being able to see ultraviolet. I know certain fish and birds that can, but what can he see beyond that?'

'Ah, Sam, don't worry about the doctor, he's a bit up himself sometimes,' Reb started to pull some information on the wall screen, until he realised the futility of it. He sighed, 'The Preialeiac are the perfect predator. They can see from ultraviolet and all the way past thermal infrared. Their hearing is impeccable, he can listen to anyone on this station from his office and I don't just mean conversations. He once called a new technician in for a check-up because the doc heard his heart murmur. They guy had just walked through the airlock.'

~*~

Back in the annals of time, the Preialeiac thought they were to be the dominant race in the universe, evolving on a most inhospitable volcanic planet with savage temperatures and continental instabilities. They were the pinnacle of evolution, even after all this time. Billions of years of evolution had not created a predator as efficient as them. Spacefaring technology opened up new feeding grounds and nearby systems fell, one after another in quick succession. The fierce warriors dropped out of ships in their thousands, falling upon cities to enslave and consume. Small to medium-sized weapons were futile upon their chitin armour; a head shot being the only sure way to kill the overly large insectoids. Anyone who faced an unravelling manifestation of the Preialeiac after he'd dropped several hundred feet to land in front of you, with their paralysis-inducing vocals tended to have a short and grim future. Each Preialeiac was savagely swinging a six-foot sabre which had literally been tempered in hell, with two pairs of long chitin armoured arms. With one long swipe of an arm they would truncate a whole patrol of armoured men, watching as they lay dying with disbelief and shock in their eyes as they tried in vain to stuff their intestine back in. To the Preialeiac it was their finest hour, fresh hordes of combatants surging upon them, feasting upon the dead and collecting grisly trophies. Suddenly disaster struck – an adversary they could not comprehend or immediately understand as they had never encountered such a thing before.

Evolving on a planet void of oxygen, they had never seen H_2O fall from the skies. Their physiology didn't suffer just from aquagenic urticaria; it was, to them, what sulphuric acid is to humans. The crack of thunder followed by a deluge from the sky initiated the death knell for millions of Preialeiac on Prontalarl IV. Those that cowered beneath shelter became easy prey for the opposing force; no quarter was given. The Preialeiac retreated to recently conquered worlds and were then pushed further back as civilisations retaliated with their new found weapon. With their ground troops decimated and their armadas stretched thin across several solar systems, it left their home world open to a devious attack. Hundreds of thousands of ice meteors were hurled across space with calculated trajectories aimed at the home world. Water was introduced to Preialei, billions of the Preialeiac became ill or died, the toxin polluting their argon oceans, streams and eventually seeping into the food chain. The fleets returned to form a barricade and for another millennia or so no one saw the Preialeiac again. Many had hoped that they had died out. To this day, few of them travel amongst the other races, fewer still mingle like the doctor.

CHAPTER 16

With Sam dressed in the BEE suit, he and Reb made their way out of the infirmary together.

'If we get time later I'll show you around the station.'

'So exactly where are we?'

'You have no name for this region of space as it is hidden by, er...' putting his finger in his ear, Sam noticed him clasping the back of it with his thumb, 'Bob, what's that galaxy called? Ah, memorable. It's far behind a galaxy you have called EGS-zs8-1.' Guiding Sam down a long windowless corridor, he commanded, 'Turn left here.'

Sam turned into an exterior corridor. It had a row of large oblong windows; Sam ran his hand over the nearest round corner. He silently assumed the laws of physics that affected Earth's aviation industry also applied to space design, that angled corners equated to weakness and stress points.

No light shone into the corridor, in fact, the opposite was true. It was so black outside that it seemed to suck the light out of the corridor. Sam had seen footage from the ISS space station and would have expected a multitude of glistening stars, not this oppressive void.

Seeing Sam's disappointment, Reb continued, 'Look to the left.'

'Holy shit!' he exclaimed involuntarily, taking a step backwards. 'Are we safe?'

'Safe is a relative word, Sam. If you mean are we in any danger from the black hole, no,' smiling that the view had caused the desired effect. 'We are in a compressed space zone similar to Minera. The station is built around the only Dia Kuklos we know of that can be redirected to other Dia Kuklos, I mentioned it the other day. The entrance opens up towards the black hole, that's why you can't see any stars. We are in a depression in space and we can't see over the rim.'

Sam nodded, studying intently the magnificent and spectacular brutal sight before him, not realising that people had literally gone mad by staring into the maelstrom, the feeling of hopelessness and insignificance overwhelming them.

'The Dia Kuklos, while being far smaller and visually unimpressive, has produced a far more profound effect on the fabric of space than the black hole. We are safe here in our own distorted bubble.'

Sam looked along the outside of the station. He could see no defined edges, the surface just tapered away.

'It's a globe, Sam, well, think of it as an onion as that is how it was built, in layers. Each layer became the outside shell upon completion. Safety first in space, the mantra is 'keep it simple, keep it safe'. If we have a hull breach, we can safely fall back to the next layer until it can be repaired. There are around 3000 personnel here today. It can be self-sustainable for up to 30,000, it can house 250,000 and 300 are always at the ready to deploy at any point in time. We can get them through a Dia Kuklos and to any destination within the Universe within twenty-four hours. The expanding outer edge is problematic as we have not discovered any new Dia Kuklos for a long time.'

The ever-so-slowly expanding influence of the ISPAW increased like the expanding surface of an inflating balloon, causing the frontier to increase in size exponentially. Council rules mandated that no expansion past a system was possible until that system was either fully integrated into the ISPAW or quarantined. Systems with non-spacefaring and technologically immature inhabitants were cordoned off with a series of semi-manned war satellites. This was to prevent any outside influences as much as to prevent the inhabitants getting out as they developed. They could not be allowed to wander about the relatively peaceful interior of council space. Not all races were benevolent and welcomed contact and the chance to become an equal member state. Those too had to be enclosed, entrapped within their own system.

Systems on the periphery had to be protected from external sources; frequently wars broke out with hitherto unknown species. If diplomatic resources failed to find an answer to the conflict, the ISPAW would bring the full force of its might to bear. Crushing the military and governing bodies of invading systems and surrounding the planets with satellites, it would scour them with prohibitive technology and send forth a hail of hellfire down upon the planet and into the planet, whenever it found it. Those inhabitants were free to live a non-spacefaring, non-warmongering life for evermore, only they were planet bound. The satellites and restrictions would only be removed if the ISPAW had expanded past that particular system. They wished to join the ISPAW and at least ten generations had lived and ruled the planet peacefully.

Ground troops would only ever be used on ISPAW member planets to bolster the native ranks and defend the inhabitants. The Shock Troops were always the first to arrive into the hot zones, those being the hardened criminals that had chosen not to go into solitary confinement on the terraforming planets or had taken a quicker death sentence. These less than honourable men found honour and bonds of trust amongst their comrades. They were honed to become even more hardened killers. Those were the disposable troops, the meat for the grinder, cannon fodder. Life expectancy was low even with all the armour they wore. Few made it to the thirteenth year, none made it intact, cyborg and robotics parts were a common sight. Many thought it a blessing to receive faster legs, stronger arms or even sharper eyes after an injury. None voiced the thoughts of going AWOL, there were no physical guards watching over the Shock Troops as none were needed. If any strayed from the battle zone or if the implanted cameras took footage of treasonous acts, or even became damaged in the fight, the soldier would simply cease to be. Built-in safeguards would trigger. The first being a simple but small explosion in the cranium with the result that the pressure of liquefied brain matter would push the eyes out of their sockets. Two redundancy measures would also trigger, the first one being that a toxin would be released into the blood stream and the second would be the reinforcing spinal implant that made the trooper stronger would sever key vertebrae. Surprisingly, many of the troopers found religion with the GCR being the most popular. It didn't matter which god or deity you believed in as long as you truly believed and were willing to sacrifice yourself for the good of others. The ISPAW religion would embrace you and give you support. As every planet and culture had its own religion, the GCR stated that they were all more or less correct but they were all multiple facets of a greater divine truth that we were not privy to. It also reminded the races that each religion was also man's (or species') interpretation of events and man is fallible, even making gods in our own image. Studies had shown that ancient and modern text deviated dramatically. This acceptance and active encouragement to study all doctrines had helped to create the biggest religious body across the universe.

After the Shock Troops entered the fray, the normal troopers would arrive to sanitise the now softened area. If more help was required after using the heavy hammer of the Shock Troops, the scalpel-like tactics of the Universal Military Police were called in. Police in name but they were highly skilled military personnel, sectioned off into specialised surgical strike teams. They were efficient, quick, quiet and very deadly. The few who were like Reb acted in smaller cohesive teams. These were the modern day ninja assassins, going where none would think to go.

Looking out of the window Sam performed a small, almost embarrassed jump from the tips of his toes. 'You have artificial gravity?' It was half question and half statement. Sam was berating himself for not picking up on it earlier, but then so much had happened in such a short time frame. The doctor had mentioned something about gravity outside of the medical room and he even had endured what the doctor had called gravity training. He'd thought the suit was restricting his movement, not that they were altering gravity – until now he hadn't even realised he was in space on a real space station.

'I am sure Doc must have mentioned it.' Reb took a disc out of his pocket. It was similar if not the same as the one he had used on the tavern table. The Minerans had long ago mastered non-metallic electronics, so as to allow their technology to pass through the Dia Kuklos. Tossing it up in the air in front of Sam he proclaimed, 'We can micro manage gravity in any of our structures or vehicles.' The small silver disk floated in front of Sam. Sam nudged it with his finger and it floated freely away.

'You can do this?'

'No,' this was said with a smile. 'I have worked with Bob for so long that I no longer need to request his input; he knows what I am doing and we act in unison. He simply contacted engineering to perform this display for you.' He placed his hand a few inches below the disc and it fell into his palm. 'Without this micromanagement, you would never have been able to throw Timon into the cell. He would simply have been too heavy to move, with his natural weight and the fact that whenever we go indoors we are always subject to Minera's normal gravity to prevent muscle loss and osteopenia.'

'How? This would be the holy grail for our space flights.'

'You're decades away from it, Sam, but it's so simple your scientists will wonder why they didn't stumble upon it earlier. Every piece of rock floating through space has a gravitation force. The strength of this force depends on its mass. How hard can it be to emulate that?'

Allowing Sam several minutes to take in the view, Reb finally prompted him to move along. 'Come on Sam, we need to make a move. The captain is eager to get going.'

The meeting was being held in a clone of the room in Minera. He was surprised at the amount of wood in the office, the parts of the station he had seen were utilitarian. The doctor's infirmary was filled with storage cupboards and apparently lots of charts and readouts. The corridors, whilst larger, could have been off any military ship he had been on. Sterile-looking steel walls and bulkheads, the sturdy bulkhead doors didn't have the usual metal wheel to lock it in place as they, like the doctor's door, slid silently into the walls. There was carpet, a thick natural fibre-looking brown carpet. That was as far as Sam's knowledge went as he had never had to buy one.

'Take a seat people,' the captain bellowed as he entered behind Sam carrying an armful of files and folders. 'We have a lot to discuss and before we leave I want a plan of action.'

Seating himself next to Lieutenant Kallistrate, the captain was positioned at the far side of the table from Sam. Remarkable really, he thought to himself, to have been dragged out of your comfort zone, your ignorant little bubble of existence, to have been manipulated, shot, rebuilt, introduced to the doctor and yet still maintain some decorum. He's either intelligent, calm and analytical to have taken it in, as Reb suggested or he was an imbecile coasting in uncertainty. We'll test his mettle before the week's out.

'I have taken the liberty of printing out the major details as Sam's here,' indicating with the corner of a file, 'and as humans can't see the full spectrum of our displays.' He slid a folder across the table to those seated. 'We are still waiting for the doctor, but we can proceed. Nik, what do you have and take it from the beginning.'

Nik slid a sheet of paper to each participant in turn. 'I'll deal with the events at the house first. We all know the perpetrator. We have little to add and I have summarised the details on the sheet. He was and still is Urser Moorc who is still alive and well in prison. The authorities have agreed to keep him under surveillance, begrudgingly as we have not explained why. The temporal degradation indicates he came through the Dia Kuklos,' holding up his hand to stifle the questions that started to pour in from all but Sam, 'please let me finish, more disturbing is that he was teleported to the house through the Dia Kuklos.'

'Impossible! This is ridiculous!' expelled a uniformed man that Sam did not recognise.

Sam leaned over to Reb, 'Teleporters don't exist, then?'

'On the contrary, they're pretty fundamental to our manufacturing industry for moving goods around internally. No sane person has used a teleporter to move a living being for, er, I can't think of a point in history that we did. Every planet, ship and building has a basic interference generator to prevent unauthorised teleportation. When the technology was initially created a few millennia ago, crime became rife. As you can imagine, a criminal flies by, teleports your valuables, flies off, and no one knows where the object or person went. They're so easy to block that they soon became obsolete except for in controlled areas.'

Nik and the man who must be a fellow scientist were still arguing. 'Enough!' bellowed Captain Sophus. 'Ed, we invited you here out of courtesy. If you'd have released more information as we requested, this might be over by now.'

'You know I don't have the authority to release those files, Hus. I gave you what I could. It'll take weeks for the upper echelons to even read your request, let alone agreeing to release it. We both know that your system would have blocked any incoming transport,' he spat.

'What I am trying to say, if you don't mind me continuing, is that we do not know when or where this transportation came from or the technology used. I have scoured the system logs and we had some very strange energy readings at that point in time. We can block it now, but I'm not sure what or how it was done.' He looked at Ed, who lowered his head and shuffled the papers about before him. He poured himself a glass of water from the jug in the middle of the table.

'We have identified the wavelength of the incoming Dia Kuklos. We are now blocking that permanently across the network. We don't know where it is but they won't be able to connect with us again. '

Sam looked at the paper that Nik had passed across, the graphs and energy readings being indecipherable gibberish to him.

'The weapon used to shoot Sam and the communications device fitted on top were made in Minera.' He paused for the impact of this statement to take hold. 'Analysis shows that it has the energy signature of one of our manufacturing units, it must have been left in the building sometime prior to Reb arriving. Whoever the traitor is, and I don't use that word lightly, traitor it must be, whoever they are, they have covered their tracks professionally, it might take months to piece it all together. Oh the weapon's comms' unit bounced off a human satellite, so the trail is cold but not dead. We are looking for the incoming signal via the Solar System Cordon Arrays, to see if we can triangulate.' Looking at Sam, 'Did anyone mention the satellite system surrounding your solar system?'

Sam nodded. 'The doctor mentioned it briefly.'

'The second incursion was just as elaborately planned on the inside, only let down by the poor choice of personnel. The doctor will report any new findings on those. The weapons where a mixture of planet-side, readily available eastern European assault rifles. I doubt we will learn much from their trail, but I have people working on it. The weapons were obviously not bought for that particular mission, as they had to quickly adapt the weapons for the sheer size of the soldiers hands. They used the secondary entrance, which has now been permanently sealed, I might add. I'll explain a little for Sam's benefit: the compressed special areas tend to create mountainous regions on the outside, it's thought to be an effect of the initial explosion, the epicentre always has a mountain too. There is a small hole at the top of ours, erm, think of it as a teardrop shaped area; most of it is inaccessible due to the mountains. We have two passes in Minera. One at the village, as you know, and one near some remote trails. We disguise the entrances to prevent accidental observation and make it difficult to approach. Sadly, this didn't deter you and you set off a multitude of alarms. If you find the entrance, there are several physical barriers in place to detain you until you can be safely dealt with.' He nodded at Sam to see if this was clearing up a few things for him. Sam gave a gentle nod back.

'Someone not only disabled the interior and exterior security and monitoring systems but they disabled the barriers and incapacitated the troops there. This was ingenious; the food and water system was laced with microscopic capsules containing a strong sedative. To ensure the incapacitation of every troop at the same time, these capsules could not be digested, only absorbed into the bloodstream. They only broke down upon a certain sonic frequency played over the comms. It was outside of our hearing range, so troops could have heard it. We only know this as Akakios was called away prior to the attack and the capsules were still in his body.'

The meeting continued on for several hours going over the finer details and a large list of suspected personnel was created. It was a duplicate of the duty roster for Minera. Sandwiches and refreshments were brought in and finally the doctor was called to report on his findings.

His large frame filled the doorway and he chose to stand rather than attempt to sit on the small chair before him.

'Gentlemen,' he greeted them all. 'I do not have much more to add regarding the arm or the enhanced soldier. Further tests have shown Urser's chronological age when he dies is 107, although this does not take into account his time in the cryogenic chamber. The bodies of soldiers who foolishly ran through the Dia Kuklos heading towards space have been recovered. These were not in pristine condition; they had suffered horrendous mutilation from the presence of metal as they passed through the surface tension of the Dia Kuklos. Subsequently they suffered more burning from the unfiltered cosmic radiation; they were not close enough to the sun to prevent them from freezing thus causing further cellular damage.'

One long arm reached over Sam and a finger skewered one of the remaining sandwiches, it was tossed unceremoniously into the doctor's mouth and swallowed almost without interrupting his report. 'We have traces of pollen and pollutants from the nostrils and lungs. These indicated they were based in North Wales, which is not helpful in itself. I took the liberty of asking Nikomedes's technicians to run a scan for anomalous energy readings.' Passing a report to Nik, 'They have just sent this through.'

Nik quickly scanned the results and looked up excitedly, 'We have a lead. They didn't find any erroneous energy readings, but they did find an energy void, a null zone – someone's shielding something. The satellite photo shows what looks like a remote farm, nothing unusual, tractors, animals, buildings, there should be an energy signature emanating from it for sure.' Looking up at the doctor, 'Are these uploaded on to the system?'

The doctor predicted this request and from Sam's point of view muttered a few unintelligible words to the system computer. The centre of the room brightened up as the satellite image hung in mid-air, the doctor arranged other data to sit alongside the picture. Zooming outwards he proceeded, 'This is the original energy scan, as you can see; the surrounding areas have a varying amount of energy out puts. These,' indicating with a sharp looking finger, 'wooden poles carry energy cables above the ground. The energy emission ends at the circumference of this void.' Whilst describing this, he dug out an item from his blue doctor's jacket and tossed it to Sam.

Sam caught the glasses by reflex as he had been looking intently at the map trying to discern what they were talking about. The glasses immediately overlaid the ultraviolet information on to the map for Sam to see, albeit in an odd glowing orange colour. Sam pushed them above his eye and back to see the difference. Feeling silly for having done so, he examined the map intently. The suspect farm was located a few miles from the nearby road with the only vehicular access via an old winding driveway. A light scattering of animals and farm equipment could be seen, a hay barn, silage pit and a collection of modern and old buildings. There were twenty or so World War One style long wooden huts on the outskirts of the usual corrugated barns and a large slate roofed farmhouse sat in the middle.

'I requested a second scan a few hours later including lifeform readings.' He laid the photograph next to the original. It was exactly the same. 'The property has been arranged to pass a casual inspection, a passing glance but nothing more. As you can see, none of the animals have moved. I surmise these are simply models to fool the casual observer from the air.' Looking again at Nik, 'Your technicians have assured me they will be able to penetrate the nullification field within a standard hour. They are waiting for one of their satellites to get into position.' Looking at Sam, 'Apparently this is made difficult by your primitive space ventures, not from the risk of you observing our technology but due to the fact you have cluttered your planet with orbiting detritus, which frequently damages our hosts.'

'Drone?' Reb suggested.

'It might alert whoever is in the area,' Nik replied. 'It's safer to wait for one of the DROS to get into position.'

The Deep Reconnaissance Orbital Satellites were all surreptitiously attached to the Earth's military satellites, each cigarette-sized package having the capabilities to analyse energy emissions up to a mile below the Earth's surface. The major drawback was that they operated on a very narrow beam and so limited their usefulness as blanket surveillance. As a by-product of attaching to the Earth's military spy, they also relayed the satellite's data to the Minerans, spying on the spies as it were.

'Why haven't we noticed this area before? It's practically on our doorstep,' expelled the captain.

'Complacency! We have been here so long and in the past any outside interference had limited influence and their energy presence shone out like a blinding star. It's getting harder now; the whole planet is blanketed with millions of differing energy signatures. Spotting areas like this is, well this is actually a poor example as the lack of any energy signatures stands out. That's one of the reasons why I wanted Sam. He can investigate freely outside of our borders, especially valuable in the cities. You know we only pass cursory inspection, if one of us got hurt and taken into hospital...'

He raised his hands. 'It's more difficult now, Hus. The rules are changing as the inhabitant's progress and the ISPAW members are noticing. Bob says there are already more member races here than ever before. I'd say some are understandably worried and are keeping an eye on things. Some are more nefarious and we need to remove those.' Pointing at the map, 'These we need to eradicate ASAP.'

'Yes, you're right, Reb. I'm sorry you're finding these things out this way, Sam. We should have eased you into it. The first priority is investigating the farm, Reb that's you. Nik, keep looking for that damned Dia Kuklos. Doc, work out how they created those soldiers and trace the technology. You can't create something this big without someone knowing something.' Looking across the room to Ed, he said, 'Ed and I have a few things to discuss, the rest of you are dismissed.

CHAPTER 17

Sam munched his way through the chocolate biscuit and drank the last of his coffee as Reb continued to read Nik's report on his tablet. The tavern was quiet and Emliton had once again fallen asleep behind the bar. It was hard to imagine him as the warrior Doc had described. He and Aunt Mae, from the café, were the only two Minerans that Sam had seen who were not built like athletes or honed from pure muscle. Sam empathised with him. He'd thought that he'd seen more than his fair share of needless death and destruction, but it was nothing to what was in Emliton's file. He found it strange that active personnel files were open access to anyone on the base, or pub in this case. He'd browsed through the system on a tablet that was perched on the table in front of him; he had been informed that it had been calibrated for his poor eyesight. The history of the Minerans and the ISPAW read like a fantasy book, only much more varied and imaginative than anything he had read before. The Minerans and humans were so alike and yet so different. Most of the time they were relaxed, natural, wanting nothing more than to be growing or making things and then, bam! Stone-faced professionals with extraordinary strength and skills. He'd watched the footage of the attack, from several different angles and now realised he'd only survived due to the lack of accuracy caused by ill-suited weapons and the mystery sniper. He and Reb had been outmatched due to their Earth-based weapons, but the Minerans at the tunnel entrance were another matter. They had been clinical killing machines: most of the squad moving progressively forward utilising the SUVs as cover and attracting the majority of the enemy fire, while the others tried to outflank the enemy employing what little cover that was there. Sam looked up the specifications for the cloned Toyota as it didn't incur any significant damage during the firefight. All the cloned SUVs had been coated, including the windows and lights, with the same compound as the toxic drums. This rendered them impregnable to what the Minerans class as small arms fire, most human assault rifles would fall into this power category.

Then Apate turned up, tearing through the enemy like a tornado. She really seemed to take the invasion personally because she fought so ferociously. Sam didn't see her suffer any injury in the video, but he surmised that she must have been hurt as he smelt her perfume in the doctor's room when he gained consciousness.

Suddenly Reb tossed his tablet onto the table with enough force that Sam heard Emliton snort and awaken. Looking at Sam he proclaimed, 'I feel we have learnt all we can about the farm. It's time the two of us went for a look around. I have sent a request through to prepare a vehicle and suitable rounds for the pistols. If we are discovered, we don't want it to be a one-sided fight.'

Sam was about to rise when Reb shouted a food order

to the now awake bartender. 'Never on an empty stomach Sam, always eat and sleep when you can.'

'I wish you would take some proper weapons Reb, these peashooters are pretty limited even with the enhanced munition,' Staff Sergeant Philokrates said as he handed Reb the pistol back.

The underground firing range was brightly lit and had fifteen rows of marker posts disappearing into the distance, indicating each 100 metre section. Sam had never seen such an extensive indoor range before, nor one so quiet. They walked behind a squad of nine men firing the MPAR carbines in short bursts. No one wore ear defenders as the weapons were eerily silent. A building would periodically light up at the furthest point and explosions would occur within, as the soldiers fired the Bunker Buster rounds through the windows, the sound somehow being muffled before it could reach the firing line. Sam was grateful he had looked up the weapons specifications while in the tavern and secretly hoped that he would get a chance to play with one.

'We'll have to wait for Kappa squad to finish. These aren't as noisy as the proper Terran versions, but I still want you to wear ear defenders in here.' He handed Reb and Sam a ball of "goo" each. Reb pulled his apart and pushed each half into an ear. Feeling a little odd, Sam followed Reb's example and found the sensation of the warm but clammy goo initially uncomfortable. After a few seconds, it seemed to flow into the inner recesses of his auditory canal. It didn't block any noise at all, he could clearly hear Staff Sergeant Philokrates speaking to Reb and the hoots of laughter from the squad of soldiers.

'It might be a good time to show the newbie his wrist armaments.'

'You could be right. I was going to leave it a little

longer to give him time to acclimatise to the suit and his partner.' Reb replied.

Philokrates used a wrist mounted mini screen that had been hidden under his cuff. Five torsos began to slide down from the ceiling. 'That should be about right for the first time,' looking at Sam with a grin.

The dummies were approximately 15 metres away and about a metre apart. The last one moved erratically back and forth.

Sam looked at his gun and then Reb. Reb let out a sigh and holstered his gun beneath his coat. He then took Sam's and holstered it on the other side. Both had disappeared beneath the leathery garment and neither produced a bulge on the surface.

'I was going to leave this until you became more familiar with the BEE, but Phil's right you need to practice before we go out. Bob can you –' He never finished the sentence as he noticed Sam's BEE suit start to alter its shape. Sam hardly felt a thing; to him the interior of the suit was the same, a body hugging baby-grow. On the exterior, a jacket similar to Reb's formed, including pockets and buttons. He opened it up and found that it was still joined to the undergarment. At his sides, an empty pistol holster and magazine rings adorned the interior of each flap. His arms hung inside real sleeves and as he waggled them the material flapped, even though he knew his arms were still encased. He looked down the opening of his right sleeve and saw a layer of the BEE still snugly protecting his arm. He rolled the sleeve back to his elbow before the material refused to go any further.

'You can take the coat off if you need to, but this does reduce the effectiveness of the remaining garment. You will have to work with... Have you given your controller a name yet?' Seeing a bewildered shake of Sam's head, he continued. 'When you get time you need to converse with him or her, get to know each other and style your clothing.' Grabbing Sam's right arm he pointed it down the range. 'Point your fist at the target and clench to fire.'

Sam did so, feeling silly and not knowing what to expect. Holding his fist out in front of him, palm down, he made a sort of small punching motion.

'Ok, let's try it this way instead.' Reb casually pointed his arm in the direction of the nearest dummy, slowly made a fist with his palm down and keeping his fist still he flexed it and the forearm muscles. Instantly a dark brown dot appeared on the torso where the Mineran heart should be. Sam couldn't quite make out what it was; he looked towards Reb for clarification.

'Think of the common misconception that porcupines shot their quills at the enemy. This,' holding up his arm, 'and this,' holding the other, 'are not porcupines but they do fire quill-like projections. Bob will always choose the right one for the job and they always contain a toxin.' Pointing back at the torso, 'they also disintegrate and disappear shortly after impact to hide the fact we have a concealed weapon.'

Sam looked back at the dummy. The brown dot had vanished.

'Your turn, Sam. Point it in the general direction and fire. Bob, or whatever you call your controller, partner, contact or however you like to think of them, will do the rest. As long as you are pointing at the enemy it will auto target. Be warned, Bob never allows me to fire indiscriminately, and he will use a tranquillizer on unarmed, non-threatening opponents. If they point a weapon at me I have the authority to terminate them, but we are not murderers.'

Sam carefully replicated the procedure and felt a small

tactile feedback from the sleeve to indicate it had discreetly fired. A brown dot appeared on the target.

'Good, now fire at me. Come on don't be afraid, I just said it won't fire indiscriminately. It will not allow you to fire at friends or non-combatants.'

Sam, feeling apprehensive, pointed his arm at Reb and flexed his muscles, but nothing happened.

'Good. The BEE can only fire five or so from each arm. It can regenerate them in a couple of hours, quicker if it is absorbing energy and matter. Normally,' he said with a smile, 'in these circumstances it's feeding off incoming enemy fire.'

Sam fired another nine quills at the torsos. Each hit the Mineran heart area with precise accuracy. As he expended the last quill from each sleeve, it again performed a tactile feedback to inform him. He could, if he stared hard enough at the sleeve, discern some barely perceptible depressions where the quill had been ejected. The BEE was an exceptional piece of equipment that he was only just starting to fathom. As Reb had indicated, he needed to talk to the voice on the other side and become familiar with both jacket and partner.

'Has he tested the suit protection abilities yet?' Philokrates asked Reb.

Reb produced his pistol with a lightning fast and fluid movement and shot Sam in the chest.

'I would have preferred it if you had let me warn the squad,' Phil said with a little ire in his voice.

The squad had all stopped and were staring across at Sam on the floor. The pistol hadn't produced much noise because of the adapted propellant and built-in suppression and from Sam's perspective the whole process was completely silent due to the goo in his ears. The round exploding on Sam's chest, the slap as he hit the floor and his non-Christian expletives did attract their amused attention. It had felt like he had been hit by a sledgehammer, swung by a Norse god, while wearing steel plate armour. The pressure of the impact had been equalised over his torso.

'Nice ammo, Phil, you really ramped up the rounds fulmination and there was no pressure coming back off the target, even at this range.'

'It's not your usual amalgamation of explosives, Reb. That toy of yours does cause us a headache now and again you know, it's just so primitive. Anyhow Doc sent us the specifications of the new soldiers that you ran into and we came up with these. Luckily he still had a few bodies left in the freezer and we shot them up a little. He really enjoys it, you know. He insisted that he warm them up and refill the veins with blood to make it more realistic. The cleaners weren't too happy.'

Sam looked up at them. Reb had shot him and they were casually talking as if nothing had happened. He didn't hurt, which was a good sign; his newly developed muscles had absorbed the impact across his torso. He looked down at his coat. Thankfully it had a design that made it close and overlap even if it wasn't fastened. It was spotless, there was not a mark on it and the bullet fragments fell away as he sat up. 'You could have given me a bloody warning!'

'Why, what difference would it make to the effectiveness of the BEE?' Reb offered a hand to help Sam up. 'Phil was correct, you needed to gain confidence in your outfit. Now you know that as long as you are not hit in the face,' he pushed his finger into his hood loop and started to bring it forward to indicate to Sam how to extract it, 'then you'll be ok. Although Bob has stated that you wouldn't want to get hit by anything more powerful than one of these. I've never heard any emotion in his voice before, but I swear he's vexed with me.'

Sam spent the afternoon on the firing range. The new pistol was far superior to the one he'd lost due to Urser shooting it. There was very little recoil and like Reb's, it was practically silent. He was informed that the impact was noisier but as the round was designed to detonate in towards the body, most of the noise was muffled by the body tissue. He couldn't hear them because of the ear goo. They selectively filtered out the harmful noises while allowing speech and ambient sounds through and were far better than anything he had used before.

~*~

Reb and Sam entered the original mountainside building that Sam had originally escaped from. They did so via a garage bay and Reb drove the SUV into an underground car park. There were rows and rows of similar SUVs and some domestic vehicles. Sam recognised some of them as surveillance vehicles from his brief stay in the B&B. As Sam passed the Astra, he looked at the back box – it was shiny and new. He had childishly watched the camera footage of the vehicle returning to the hamlet after Billy had performed his little prank. Although it was not for the comedy value, he actually wanted to see and mentally measure the people who had been keeping an eye on him.

Reb led him through a stout wooden door and along a series of hallways until they came to the office of Staff Sergeant Timon.

'Reb. Didn't expect to see you here.' He gave Sam a dirty and annoyed look and then blanked him out.

'We have a small recon job at a farm an hour or so

from here. It's probably nothing more than a Member having an illegal presence on this rock, but its close proximity requires a look. Fancy tagging along? I was going to take Pat, but she's not available.'

'Ah, I suppose Sam can't act as your official backup,' he said with a slight sneer, apparently holding a grudge for Sam throwing him into the cell. 'Not up to scratch, as they say.'

'Officially, Sam is attending as an observer until he has completed his training. He is more than capable of defending himself should the need arise.'

'Ok, but I'm not taking those puny toys Reb. If we get into trouble, you'll be glad of an MPAR. When do we leave?'

'Grab your gear, we'll bring the Toyota to the exit garage and wait for you there.'

CHAPTER 18

Emliton watched as Reb and Sam finished off their meal. He sat down with a weary sigh and absentmindedly played with the torc around his neck. He looked at his old rifle hanging under the bar and brushed an imaginary speck of dust off the silvery barrel. No Mineran is ever far from his weapon. It becomes part of their very being. He could no more leave it than he could leave his leg or arm. Lifting it out of the cradle he polished its full length with his bar towel. It still felt natural in his arms after all of these years of inactivity. True, he had to fire it every month to qualify for the mandatory range proficiency, but unlike the majority of his comrades he always chose the harder distance range without the fancy scopes or the barrel extender. Ten shots with perfect accuracy accrued him more points than half an hour on the shorter ranges and enough to qualify. He didn't even have to try hard. He had gained such proficiency with his MPAR that he could have performed those shots all day with only one arm and riding a unicycle while inebriated. He'd never admit to the level of customisation he had performed on the weapon, ranging from altering the weight and balance to suit his arm length, to a plethora of enhancements to increase range, power and accuracy. The MPAR was such a versatile weapon and hardy, even though it was issued for life, it often outlived the owner. This particular rifle was passed down to Emliton by his dying great-great-great-grandfather and it was still in pristine condition. Besides the modifications, a few parts had been replaced over the years but the body was original.

He had the original barrel which was still in serviceable condition as payload was propelled via a contactless, friction-free propulsion field. He could, and had frequently performed accurate long distance shots with the basic weapon setup and he rarely used the sniper barrel extension, as he found it unbalanced and slightly cumbersome. He had secretly replaced it with one that was a fraction longer as the field nodes could produce a tighter riffling effect, adding the extra gyroscopic stability for long-range shots. The rifle's on-board computer would determine and alter the nodes power output depending on the projectile, type of target and its distance.

He found his hands were field stripping the weapon without him even thinking about it, his muscle memory taking over as he had downtime and a weapon in his hands. "A clean weapon is an efficient weapon", was the mantra that was drilled into him at the academy so many years ago. He learnt how to strip and fire the MPAR even before he needed to shave. With nimble fingers he reassembled the rifle and placed it back under the bar. He hadn't done this for a long time. Sure, he cleaned it after every range session, but he hadn't cleaned it without thinking since... well, for a long time.

He knew why. Even if he was trying to deny it. The

winds of change were all around, he could feel them. Taking on Sam to help investigate planet side infractions shouldn't have caused any ripples, but for some reason it had. His presence had caused a hitherto unknown foe to announce themselves and probably earlier than they had anticipated judging by the ill-prepared and prototype soldiers they had encountered. He might only be a barman and brewer these days, but he still kept abreast of the situations going on throughout the Universe. More so now as he had more free time to delve deeper into the archives and perform research. What he had grave suspicions about was slowly bringing him back. He had always put others before himself and core psyche was slowly forcing him out of his self-imposed melancholic reverie. There was more investigating to do, of course, he couldn't prove anything or even point the finger at any particular race, but there was a pattern forming.

He felt the band around his neck again. Many thought it was a device he had built to prevent his narcolepsy and those who knew the truth helped to propagate this illusion. It did act in this fashion but he didn't build it. He was awarded it a long time ago and every time his chin fell upon it, the ice cold sensation it produced awakened him from his nightmares. He didn't have narcolepsy, sleep was the last thing he wanted. Even when his body was crying out for it. The dreams, the horror of events long gone, the faces of those he couldn't save. Not this time, not again; he could perceive a pattern he had to heal. Not now, not at this moment, the thoughts were too new, just tiny glistening speckles of light amongst the darkest thoughts in his head, offering redemption. A chance to be whole again, a purpose. Soon, he thought. Soon!

Screech would understand. He and Emliton had stood

on so many planets back to back facing overwhelming odds, only to come out unscathed. He never could pronounce his name and was frequently reminded that his limited hearing could not black out all the sounds, tones or nuances inflected as it was pronounced. So they called him Screech back then. Only when Emliton had become ill did he also leave the battlefield. He took up medicine and psychology to try and heal his friend. This was something Emliton would never comprehend, but it showed a bond of friendship that he was eternally grateful for. No Preialeiac had ever studied medicine before. If they got hurt, they healed themselves or died. The concept of interfering with the natural order of things was alien to them. To study the physiology of alien races in order to heal them was also an abhorrent concept to the Preialeiac. Prior to them turning reclusive, they only studied others to be able to kill them efficiently. Doc, as he was known now, had never given up on him, realising after many years of study that only time would heal his wounds. That and a new sense of purpose. Is that why he had helped search through the archives and arranged for Emliton to meet and interview some of the wounded as they returned from the front? Did the doctor know, or like himself, did he suspect, or was he humouring Emliton's secret obsession? No, not that, the doctor was too honest for deception like that. He needed to talk to him soon. Not now though, not just yet.

He glanced across at the two patrons who were busily eating his BBQ Rib special and jacket potato. He'd known Reb long enough to realise he was stocking up before action. He quickly scanned the current mission roster and intriguingly found nothing for Reb and Sam. Emliton shook his head. It didn't bode well when you had to keep secrets from your fellow Minerans.

Both Reb and Sam wore the BEE suit. Sam clearly wasn't used to wearing his yet as he unconsciously fidgeted within it. A highly secret and rare piece of equipment, Minera had four suits stationed here. Was this an omen too, a gathering of forces for troubled times ahead?

The BEE suit didn't come with a manual. Each wearer would use it differently from the other, depending on their abilities, experience and primarily their dialogue and partnership with the controller. He fondled his torc again. Only the doctor and Captain Sophus knew that it was the dormant BEE suit that he used to wear. Not everything was in the Mineran public domain as Sam had been informed. Even Reb was unaware of Emliton's full history as he'd burnt out a long time before they met. He hadn't spoken to TESS for a long time. TESS was his acronym for how he thought of the suit, The ExoSkeleton Suit and what he called his contact. TESS had explained in the early days of his exploratory wearing of the BEE that their race had no concept of gender, but if Emliton preferred to think of it as a she, then he may do so. For some reason he felt better having the suit and his life controlled by a female, albeit a voyeuristic one and he would never know privacy again. Reb only scratched the surface of what the suit could do. Minerans were not very inventive and could take things at face value. Being told the suit can do X does not mean it is restricted to X and cannot perform the rest of the alphabet as well. One just had to enquire with one's controller.

Emliton had pushed his suit beyond what he thought possible in his last battle. He had fought in his depression to die and TESS and the suit had fought to keep him alive. The outer shell resembled hard ceramic for the majority of the time, saving the briefest instant to react to incoming fire compared to Reb's style of flexible material. TESS adapted it to his fighting style as she used all she had previously learned about his fighting techniques. In close quarter combat he utilised his knife more than he should as the red mist took over. TESS sharpened the ceramic edges as he elbowed and kneed his opponents, razor-shaped edges biting deep and taking huge chunks out of the short-lived enemy. He took the head clean off one soldier with a forearm to the throat. His whole arm had become a living sword. He and Screech were deep behind enemy lines; the city they were in was littered with the fallen populace. Emliton had to tell himself they were children's dolls scattered about, broken and bloody. Looking back, it obviously hadn't worked as he broke down shortly after.

The Inchethslar were brutally strong. A new unknown race from beyond the perimeter, their particle ray weapons shredded unshielded flesh off the bone like a hot knife through butter. The Shock Troops, encased within their armour, were immune to such devices and soon racked up a series of quick victories until the enemy replaced their futile armoury with a variety of explosive projectile weapons. They also reinforced them with acid throwers, armour dissolving gas and gels, and for a brief period they used a bizarre vacuum bomb which sucked nearby troops and any loose items, into the epicentre. No one knew what was meant to happen to the troops that were caught in the centre. Whatever the secondary payload was meant to do, the Shock Troops' armour provided immunity to it and they simply got up a little embarrassed and ran for cover.

The Shock Troops had seen all kinds of weapons before and were equipped for such scenarios. It just took longer to clear an area and the body count mounted.

That's where he and Screech came in, deep behind the lines, looking for the head of the beast.

Two weeks with little rest and even less sustenance he endured. Screech simply ate whomever he killed; apparently normal body fluids didn't affect him like pure water would. Emliton realised at the beginning of the second week that the suit must be transferring sustenance to him as he was not hungry, thirsty or as tired as he should have been. The blood and flesh of the opponents that inevitably splashed onto his armour was quickly absorbed into the organic material. It simply wasn't getting enough energy from the few weapons that managed to hit him. He felt godlike, invincible and fought with a masterful savagery and precision that even impressed Screech. However, for every soldier he executed he saw twenty small fragile bodies torn to bits on the floor around him. He fought like a Berserker that couldn't die when all around him lay death with its cloying, ever-present odour.

He collapsed as he slew the last warrior in an underground bunker, the head of the proverbial beast. He didn't consciously notice it at the time but the commander of this invading arming was subtly different from the rest and mostly he was silent as the twelve-inch friction free blade eviscerated him. He also hadn't previously noticed that none of the combatants had uttered a single word. Not that you normally swapped pleasantries as you slew a guy but war cries were frequent, normally along the lines of 'Die, you...' followed by various profanities about their lineage.

Later on, as he was recovering in hospital on home world Minera, apparently a decorated hero, he learnt that Screech had called in back up. With the intel they found on the command bunker computer systems, they soon cleared up the now disorganised foe. It was never discovered how they intended to exit from the planet as no spacefaring transport ships had remained with the vast army, and looking back at it, it was possibly a one-way mission from the start. It was also never discovered where they had come from or why they attacked a seemingly insignificant planet full of a highly intelligent, baby-like populace. It was written up, and possibly incorrectly Emliton thought, as an unprovoked territorial invasion. As the expansion of the outer perimeter is an excruciatingly slow process, that information might not come to light for many generations.

As Emliton mulled these memories over, he watched Reb and Sam leave silently. They too were enshrouded in their own deep dark thoughts.

The newly kindled fire within wasn't burning bright enough to eradicate Emliton's depressive shadows yet. Thoughts and ideas continued to tumble around and parts of the puzzle would re-materialise from previous research. He didn't understand how to piece them together yet, but he would if he was given enough time. Each thought fanned the embers of the fire, each one promising to make it roar, each one making him angry.

CHAPTER 19

They exited into the Minera hamlet via a discreet garage door attached to one of the rear business premises. None of the lorry drivers who saw the vehicle leave took any notice. Sam looked into the café and saw another young female assisting the matronly Aunt Mae. The truck drivers all had huge platefuls of steaming food and more than one turned their head as the waitress passed by. Sam didn't have a watch anymore and he realised that he had lost track of both time and date. He gauged that it must be getting close to closing time as the sun was behind the rock face and producing long shadows.

'It serves as a catchment for curious wayfarers and the drivers by giving them a place to loiter while we control their movement. Don't let Aunt Mae's friendly persona deceive you, she's lovely but she is as tough as any of us. There's a body scanner hidden in the heater above the door and you would be surprised at what some drivers carry.'

The journey was uneventful with Timon periodically speaking to Reb in another language. Reb ignored this by replying in English or, as he had phrased it previously, bastardised Unilang 1. Besides this, the journey's silence was only punctuated by the satellite navigation unit describing route directions. Timon sat in the front with Reb driving, having pulled rank over Sam and he pushed the seat as far back as it would go to restrict Sam's leg room. He simply changed seats to sit behind Reb, which gave him more opportunity to study the only discourteous Mineran he had met.

They drove past the closed farm gate with its long meandering drive, the roofs of the farm buildings could be seen in the distance, and it all looked quiet and peaceful. Reb had decided to park on a lane two miles behind the farm and walk cross country to the rear for his reconnaissance. They followed a public footpath for the first half a mile and then deviated into a small gulley created by the swift-flowing stream of mountain water. At certain points they had to move within the stream itself as the gully sides became narrow and steep. Sam developed another appreciation for his BEE as the built in boots kept him dry and warm in the chilly water. He didn't really care how Timon was feeling, the man's rude demeanour was starting to irritate him now. Humans might not be to the same intellectual or physical level as the Minerans, but that didn't give him the right to be bitchy all the time.

The gulley broke out into wide sections as the now shallow, fast-moving stream caressed the pebbled bed. Reb indicated for them to settle on the gentle grass-covered slope. Pulling out a small pair of binoculars, he slowly eased his head above the embankment. The long grass this side of the electric fence, out of reach for the bovine in the field, shielded his face from view.

'It'll be sundown at 6:30. If we wait till dark we can

follow the hedge on the left to prevent us from being silhouetted and make our way behind the silage pit towards those old billets. They're probably just chicken houses now. If we're careful we should be able scope out the farm from there first.' He passed the binoculars to Sam. Timon had his own and having seen enough gently squirmed his way down and out of sight, his left hand keeping the MPAR close by and ready to bear at all times.

'Why would aliens, and I mean no offence, need chickens?' Sam looked at Reb for the answer.

'Bear in mind how difficult it would be to initially get onto this planet without setting off the cordon around your system. It also means they have to be pretty self-sufficient. It makes sense if you're settling in for the long haul to produce as much as you can yourself. The less interaction you have with the natives, the less chance you have of being exposed.'

'How can they get past the cordon?'

'Well, it's old and not really a military grade cordon. Initially it was set up to block incoming signals and warn off the odd ship that passed by. There was nothing here in those days and you are in the middle of nowhere. All of the satellites were upgraded at the turn of the century, but as a non-spacefaring planet, you have not been annexed because of your current aggression. It's more political pressure and laws that keep the ISPAW members out; this type of incursion should never have happened.'

'Every system is worried you will all go nuts again and that they will have to waste valuable resources and effort incinerating this miserable planet...again. You do know the story, right?' The look of glee in Timon's face was sickening.

'Doc has informed me about the two previous inhabitants of Earth and how your communication systems interfered with their brains, yes!'

'Good, because if it weren't for the Protected Species label that the council have put on you, this planet would be a cinder again.'

'Give it a rest, Timon, yes there are misgivings within the council, but they would never sanction such actions against a primitive and non-threatening world,' Reb rebuked Timon.

'Why do you hate Earth so much?' Sam enquired while trying to keep his voice down. He was still examining the old wooden structures through Reb's high-tech binoculars. A series of buttons on the right-hand side grip altered the zoom spectrum frequency. He was currently viewing the blue looking building through the thermal setting. The only warm areas he could see belonged to the randomly spaced animals roaming around and the silage pit as the grass fermented. None of the vehicles had been used for a while and even the parts of the house that he could see offered no warm glow.

'I don't hate your planet, it's a highly prized resource which is sadly being destroyed by an idiotic ignorant populace. What you don't understand is that evolution here has been extremely erratic, with two mass extinctions. It's almost as if the planet or evolution is trying as many permutations as possible hoping one will survive. Even in your own species there are so many different traits and variations. You are all unpredictably dangerous and you will turn on the rest of the Universe once you discover space flight. It's in your nature.'

'Sam's ability to think at an odd tangent to the rest of us, to be able to coalesce random facts into a working theory and to take leaps of faith, is what we need.' Reb slid down alongside Timon and the heated discussion was performed at a loud whisper. 'They could be a valuable asset and you know it, that what's galling you so much. They're primitives now, but they have the ability for greatness.'

'Yeah, right. With their life span a very brief greatness.' Timon looked at Reb. 'I'll scout further up the stream, see where we can come out near that hedge later.'

They waited until dusk was nearly over to move out, when the darkness was not quite night time. The hedge had been properly maintained and trimmed to retain a decent height and thickness. They had to crouch nonetheless to prevent their heads from being silhouetted against the sky line. Timon took point with his carbine, Sam second and Reb taking the rear. As Reb hadn't drawn his weapon yet Sam followed his lead, though he felt oddly naked performing a recon in unknown territory without drawing his firearm. The half a mile trek to the silage pit took less than ten minutes. After a visual inspection of the preceding area, they prepared to quickly jog across to the first wooden building.

Timon pushed the barrel of his MPAR into Reb's back. 'Keep your arms low and where I can see them, Reb. Same for you, human.'

'Timon!'

'Stay still, this'll blast a hole through that suit of yours and you know it.'

'What are you doing?' Reb slowly turned around and faced Timon, who stepped back.

'This is not personal and I respect you enough to let you go when it is all over, but they want him!' He didn't wave the gun or even flick his eyes at Sam. He remained solidly fixed on Reb.

Two large soldiers appeared from behind the silage pit. Even in the poor light Sam could make out that they were carrying a modified Atchisson Assault Shotgun with the

32 cartridge drum beneath. They pointed these at Sam and Reb, holding them casually near the hip. For a normal human the recoil would tear the gun from their hand. Sam didn't think it would be an issue for these genetic mutants.

'Why do they want him so badly, Timon?'

'That's not my problem, Reb, I didn't ask.'

'So you're taking orders from these now?' indicating the brutes behind him.

'No, these are just the fruit of their endeavours. You were right by the way, the vermin that live on this planet do have abilities that are useful. They're the quickest sentient breeders we have ever come across and their genetic code is apparently easy to manipulate.' Timon stepped back again and started to walk around his captives giving them a wide cautious berth. Standing between his new companions he continued. 'There is a war coming, Reb. Their masters are from beyond the edge of the ISPAW sphere. We haven't expanded anywhere near their worlds yet, but they have found us. Can you imagine these in full armour with MPARs? Even our Shock Troops would crumble at the sight of them.'

Timon looked forlorn then. 'I'm sorry Reb, I lied before, I didn't want to be the one who killed you. You are my friend, but they promised to bring her back. I miss her so much.' Tears of conflict ran down Timon's face as he lowered his weapon. 'Goodbye, Reb.'

Two flesh rending sounds punctuated Timon's sentence as a red hole appeared on each of the brute's foreheads. They stood there for what seemed an eternity. Sam watched bemused as a trickle of really thick blood seeped out of the wound. Almost with slow motion grace the legs of the brutes gave way. The command to stand rigid was no longer being sent to them. Both fell forward onto their knees, their arms sagged under the weight of the seven kilogramme weapons and they finally fell face down into the short grass. Sam realised he was becoming immune to viewing the inside of someone's head as the two gaping maws steamed into the night air.

Timon brought his weapon up to bear and just as quickly it fell to the floor. He looked down horrified at the bleeding stumps where his arms had been. His hands were still cradling the MPAR as it lay by his feet.

'Staff Sergeant Timon, it is my solemn duty to inform you that you have lost the right to bear arms, pun intended. You are hereby stripped of your service name and will henceforth be known as Aeschylus.' Neither Sam nor Reb had drawn their weapon yet, but Reb pointed his fist at the non-Timon as he spoke and shot him with a quill. At this distance Sam assumed it would have had enough force to pass straight through a body, even one as muscular as Timon /Aeschylus. He could only surmise that as it stood out proudly from Aeschylus' chest, Bob had fine control over the amount of force he used. He really must spend some time getting to grips with the BEE suit. He thought to himself, what am I to call him? I can't call him Bob as well.

Aeschylus looked at Reb with a pained query in his silently weeping eyes.

'Something to stop you going into shock and a coagulant to prevent you bleeding out until the medics arrive. Old friend, I do not envy what lies ahead of you now, but know this, Nikomedes says the fire at your house has a temporal signature similar to Urser's remains. They caused it, probably by accident as they were trying to send Urser through years further on.'

The now Aeschylus fell to his knees and sobbed, broken and alone.

Apate stepped silently between Sam and Reb and struck the kneeling figure in the face with the butt of her sniper rifle, breaking his nose. 'I told you the last time I broke your nose that if you threaten him I would fricking kill you. Enjoy your stay in Hell little man, for where you are going you will crave for a swift exit.' She was wearing her BEE suit, only on her it looked amazing, accentuating her natural lithe curves. For some reason Sam thought of the suit leaving her body smooth and hairless.

He forced his gaze away and became aware of shadow clad figures carrying MPARS creeping past them. Sam counted at least a hundred in small squads making their way to the farm. A medic appeared alongside the prone figure and sprayed the slowly weeping stumps with a foam that formed an emergency bandage and moved onwards with the rest of his comrades.

'You could have forewarned me about this,' Sam said, looking at Reb and gesturing with his hands.

'I wasn't sure and part of me wanted to be wrong. Partly because I wouldn't wish what's going to happen to him on anyone. The interrogation techniques that will be used, even if he freely confesses and tells us everything will need to be verified and that can only be done with a scour. It's a process that compels the subject to narrate their memories. It's slow, it hurts and you never really come out of the process the same.' He placed a hand on the fallen's head. 'I am sorry old friend.'

~*~

Somewhere, in the not too distant future, a strong female hand gently caressed the bald head of a tired-looking warrior. He was lying prone behind a weapon designed to propel the Spica Sagitta. The floor around him was strewn with corpses dressed in a blood-red uniform. Not the bright, cheerful red of normal, healthy blood, but the dark hue of deoxygenated dying blood. They had all fought bravely, all from a multitude of species but all genetically engineered, each race having a particular trait that was enhanced by their masters, be it brains or brawn. The majority of the soldiers looked similar to the one on the other side of the Dia Kuklos, though clearly the process had been refined and perfected. Not once did the enemy seek clemency and no quarter was offered as the two figures had fought their kind before and understood that they were conditioned to obey orders until death.

He had just fired the last arrow in a body of one of the fallen; the fire in the tunnel partially obscuring his view.

The scene they were viewing was chaotic and yet comical at the same time. The Dia Kuklos through which they were watching was dilating time just as Nikomedes had predicted all those years ago.

Watching the naked body of a man being unpinned from a large metal block, the female commented with a grin, 'You've done all you can, love, we need to move. I remember that hairy chest, how cute!'

ACKNOWLEDGEMENTS

I would like to thank the following people for helping to make this book happen.

Cath Roberts for her continued support during the writing process, beta reading and feedback.

Sue Miller from TeamAuthorUK for support, proof reading and editing and Ellen Parzer for the cover creation.

Michelle Roberts for beta reading and feedback.

THANK YOU FOR READING!

Dear Reader,

I hope you enjoyed this book; **Mineran Influence**. I have to tell you that I enjoyed writing it and I love the characters of Sam, Erebus, Apate and the Doctor. When **Mineran Influence** was originally released as an eBook, I had so many people asking 'What's next for Sam and the others?' and 'Can we have it on paperback?'. Well, stay tuned as there are many adventures to come and in the future the series will always be published in paperback.

I have so many ideas for future of Sam and the gang that, even while I am writing book three at the moment, my head is awash with ideas for the rest of the series.

As an author, I love feedback from you the reader, and in honesty, it is you the reader that will encourage me to further explore the ISPAW universe with its many diverse species and dangers. So here is the part where I am going to ask you, the reader for a small favour.

Book reviews can be tough to come by these days; often readers do not realise how important a review can be to an author. In truth, it is you the reader who has the power to make or break a book with your reviews. If you have the time, please could you leave a review on Amazon for this book. You can search for the book page by name or you can find it via my Amazon Author Profile: http://amzn.to/2eVIwSK

Thank you for reading this book, and I hope you like the next in the series **Mineran Conflict**. As a small gesture I have included the first paragraph in the extras section.

In gratitude

ABOUT THE AUTHOR

P N Burrows was born in England and raised in rural Wales. Phil has worked in a variety of roles over the years from IT Consultant to a Business Advisor. In his spare time, he loves to read and particularly enjoys crime thrillers. He also enjoys working his way through a comprehensive bucket list that he and his partner have created, they can frequently be found dancing the Lindy Hop. As an author Phil is a proud member of Team Author UK, a small organization whose goal is to help Indie Authors like himself.

Web: www.pnburrows.com

FB: www.facebook.com/PNBurrows

Twitter: @pnburrows

BOOK 2 - COMING IN 2017
MINERAN CONFLICT

Having enlisted with ISPAW's quasi-military Universal Police and trained with the Minerans for a year, Sam is sent on his first mission. 'It will be safe and easy,' they said. No it wasn't, and Sam's training didn't cover what happened!

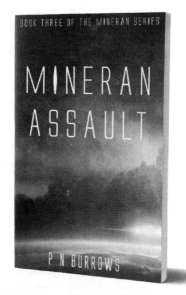

BOOK 3 - COMING IN 2017
MINERAN ASSAULT

While the team frantically search for Sam, he struggles to survive and to evade capture. The traitor and the truth behind ISPAW's mysterious and vengeful nemesis is uncovered.

BOOK 2 - COMING IN 2017
MINERAN CONFLICT

CHAPTER 1

Sam had his back to the dirty block cinder wall and watched as the shadows of those on the other side played across the rectangle of sunlight that streamed through the doorway. He was listening intently to the conversations and was secretly excited and dismayed at the same time, as he hadn't expected to find so many here. Judging by the names he could hear being called out Sam was certainly outnumbered and physically outmatched. He recognised a few of the names from the files he had read prior to this assignment and knew that, even with the strength-enhancing abilities of his BEE suit, he wouldn't be able to hold his own in a one-to-one confrontation. These guys were bigger, faster and stronger than him, and more importantly, they had survived this long because they were professionals.

Sam looked at the concrete stairway leading down to the first floor of the engineering unit, the updraft bringing fresh air in from outside and hopefully an advanced warning of a strange scent if a patrolling guard decided to enter the building. It would take too long for any backup to arrive and if he left it any longer, he ran the risk of being discovered or the meeting ending.

Sam wasn't in the movies; he could not enter the room and demand that they raise their hands, well appendages, of various sorts, and surrender. That would inevitably lead to a fist fight, after one of the perpetrators knocked his gun to one side. Rule number one of villainy was to fight dirty and he couldn't expect anyone on this planet to understand or abide by the Marquess of Queensberry rule book. Now was not a time for chivalry, foolishness or bravery, he had a critical mission and failure would have dire consequences. With a wicked grin, he took out his secret weapon from his pocket. Nikomedes had designed it to Sam's specification and proving that the Mineran did have a sense of humour, had vaguely fashioned it after the 1920s MK II grenade. Sam pushed the safety slide up and sideways in an L shape to uncover the activation fingerprint reader that was located at the top of the palm-sized pineapple. Placing his thumb to activate the device, he waited for the ever so discreet vibration to indicate it was ready to throw. Sam had specifically instructed Nik that he didn't want lights, beeps, pins, clasps or anything that might alert his quarry.

He tossed the grenade through the doorway, shuffled sideways a few feet and put his fingers in his ears. The hand-grenade moved in a slow, gentle arc from Sam's toss. Within milliseconds the on-board computer analysed its trajectory, the room's dimensions, contents and placement of all organic matter. It calculated the precise time to explode to cause maximum impact to all organic lifeforms. Milliseconds before exploding, it ejected thousands of micro beads in a pattern that it had governed to be the most potent to pepper the room's inhabitants. The blast from the explosion was immense; it carried the minuscule spherical objects out in front of the blast wave and threw everything around like leaves in an autumn wind. Sam was surprised at how quiet the grenade was, he felt rather than heard the explosion. Peeking around the door frame, he saw the sun covered floor had become peppered by the fluorescent green balls as the dye expanded. Finally, the room settled back down as the last of the flung items crashed to the floor.

Stepping through the door, Sam surveyed the carnage and with a quiet chuckle, he muttered to himself about how Nik had done a wonderful job. Seven bodies lay strewn and inert across the room. Sam walked up to each in turn and shot them in any exposed flesh that he could see. It was overkill he knew, but it was better to play safe with these guys. The green gel that the grenade had thrown out was designed to humanely incapacitate up to ninety-eight per cent of all known life forms. The problem arose when you encountered the remaining two per cent or came across a species that could metabolise the chemical composition quicker than anticipated. Sam's tranquilliser gun was programmed to recognise all of the Sphere's species, adapt the payload and thus guarantee the subject remain unconscious for at least an hour.

He stood back to review the scene. As he had requested, the gel balls had concentrated in the area where the victims had been positioned, but more importantly, the grenade had also spread a fine mesh of gel across the remainder of the room. As long as there was a complete fluorescent green mesh covering everything, Sam could rest assured that no one had moved, i.e. that he hadn't found one of the two per cent who might now be lurking somewhere to clobber him.

He stealthily looked out of the dirty windows to ensure the patrolling guards had not been alerted. Thankfully their perimeter was far enough away for the maelstrom not to have been heard. Sam removed the other present he had received from Nik and proceeded to process each of the seven bodies in turn. Laying them on their sides, he pulled their arms behind their backs and sprayed the foaming compound from the canister around their wrists and hands. The foam was visually not too dissimilar to builders' foam, although this version set hard as a diamond and it could only be dissolved with the correct sequence of enzymes. Even with the added strength of the BEE suit, it would be unable to break out the polymer, so as a precaution, Sam had insisted the BEE suit absorb a small amount of the enzyme in case he became entangled in the foam himself. He performed the same encapsulating process on their legs and then effectively hog-tied them with a strand going from arms to legs; these were ruthless and unbelievably robust entities after all.

As Sam dragged the last body in line with the rest, he heard a loud thud behind him. Whipping around with his pistol drawn he saw a patrol guard slumped on the floor of the doorway. He looked back to the window and noticed a three-inch circular hole in the glazing, 'She says, "you're welcome", Sam,' the voice vibrated through his body until it hit his auditory canal to mimic sound vibrations for Sam to hear.

Putting his middle finger in his ear he said, 'Tell her thank you.'

Apate was half a mile away on one of the rooftops and had covered his back with her usual precision. To avoid the noise of the glass shattering which would, of course, raise an alarm, she was using a precursor laser on her silent MPAR sniper rifle. The on-board system analysed the glass composition, calculated the distance, the dissipation radius and the energy required to dissolve the glass ahead of the bullet. This left an elegant hole in the glass and a body on the floor; it also meant Sam would have to buy Apate dinner as he had now lost their private wager.

Replacing his finger in his ear, which was an unnecessary habit he had picked up from Reb when he was speaking to his controller, he proclaimed: 'Room's clear!'

'She says, "you know they are going to be annoyed when they come round".' The vocal vibrations were now only emanating down his wrist and into his ear; this was much more pleasant than feeling his whole body vibrate when his controller spoke through his suit. They had come to an agreement, in that his collar would gently vibrate to indicate that non-urgent communication was required.

He looked at the bodies trussed up on the floor, five of which were similar in build to his own, trim but muscular and of average height. The other two were massive brutes, their eyes wrapping around to their temples which gave them a much wider angle of view and also helped to define them as either Fleelrok or Fleelrak from the Fleelks'is's solar system. Both races had a common distant ancestry who colonised the system a millennia or so ago, but for some reason that Sam couldn't remember, their home world had died, orphaning the two planets with limited and dwindling resources.

Over time, as irreplaceable parts wore out, they lost the capability of space flight and became isolated. Eventually, evolution on the separate planets had altered them to a form better suited to their environments.

The Fleelrak'is, being nearer the sun, is quite arid and suffers from violent dust storms for six months of the year. This caused the inhabitants to develop a particulate filtering system similar to gills under their arms, a third and fourth set of eyelids and for some reason, their genital moved from their lower legs to their inner thighs. Sam was not intrigued enough to investigate further, as either race was more than a match for him in unarmed combat.

Returning to a familiar figure on the floor he decided to add extra foam to encase the whole of the man's legs, 'That's because you were not meant to be here, Reb,' he said out loud, not that anyone besides his controller could hear him. He put his finger in his ear for the final time and stated, 'I am standing down, training scenario complete.'

He sat down behind the desk and put his feet on the polished wooden top. He could understand his friends and colleagues travelling from Earth back to planet Minera wishing to attend his passing-out training scenario. What he hadn't expected was for some of them to participate. If he hadn't come up with the idea of the grenade, it would have been him on the floor trussed up like a hog. The lesson, this time, was to never underestimate what is around the corner, 'Boing Flip boys,' he thought to himself, 'Boing Flip.'

Sam pondered that it was unusual that Emliton and the doctor hadn't come to see him. He'd seen a lot of them over his intensive twelve-month training regime and had come to consider them, along with Erebos, Nikomedes, Captain Sophus, Alcaeus & Xenophon, as trusted friends and mentors. For some reason they had all taken a personal interest in his development and continued to support him while he was away from Earth, often training him far beyond the required training syllabus and in their own time. All bar Em and the doc had arrived yesterday for the ceremony tomorrow, although thank goodness the doc hadn't been in the room as he was definitely immune to the grenade's gel.

Feeling his collar buzz, he fingered his ear. 'Pat says if you don't wipe that smug look off your face she will shoot you with a tranquilliser as well.'

How could he have forgotten Apate, she most of all had carried him through all of this. When the universe seemed to overwhelm him with its monsters, she always showed him the beauty it contained, often just by being there herself. He looked out of the window towards a tall warehouse in the distance and smiled with genuine affection. She would shoot too he thought, just before he plunged into unconsciousness and slipped off the chair.

Novel Websites

We provide affordable websites for novelists.

Our author package is specially designed to aid writers in marketing their books. We are also authors, so we know how expensive and time-consuming marketing a book can be.

Affordable, no hidden monthly fees!

Friendly and approachable service.

www.novel-websites.co.uk
phil@novel-websites.co.uk